**The Urbana Free Library**

To renew: call **217-367-4057**
or go to **urbanafreelibrary.org**
and select **My Account**

# PRAISE FOR DAVID BERGEN

"Bergen's best writing evokes the absence of what has been lost
and, even more terribly, what is not there to be found."
—*The Globe and Mail*

"David Bergen is, simply put, one of our best modern writers."
—Jury citation, 2009 Writers' Trust Timothy Findley/
Marian Engel Award

"With his thoughtful dialogue, Bergen makes the characters'
heartache seep off the page." —*TIME*

"Bergen's characters move and breathe, demonstrating
the delicate balance between hope and despair, salvation
and damnation." —*Toronto Star*

"In *Leaving Tomorrow*, Bergen gives us another richly observed life."
—*Winnipeg Free Press*

"*Leaving Tomorrow* is pure pleasure. It . . . deserves to take its place
alongside such mid-western Canadian classics as *Who Has Seen the
Wind* and *A Complicated Kindness*." —*The Globe and Mail*

"*Leaving Tomorrow* is a contemplative novel full of the hope that comes with youth, but in the end it becomes clear that like life, the journey is the real destination." —*Toronto Star*

"This is a moving and engaging novel of grief and loss, impeccably written and fully imagined."
—*Toronto Star* on *The Matter with Morris*

"A beautifully composed, unflinching and harrowing story. Perhaps the best fiction yet to confront and comprehend the legacy of Vietnam."
—*Kirkus Reviews* (starred review) on *The Time in Between*

"David Bergen is a master of taut, spare prose that's both erotic and hypnotic. Set mostly in modern-day Vietnam, *The Time in Between* is a deeply moving meditation on love and loss, truth and its elusiveness, and a compelling portrait of a haunted man, Charles Boatman, and his daughter who seeks to solve the mystery of his disappearance."
—MIRIAM TOEWS

"*The Time in Between* is about how children inherit their parents' ghosts and the elusive nature of grace. It also makes a stunning connection between the wars that are fought out in the world, and the ones that cleave families in private. Ravishingly told and deeply felt, it's a huge accomplishment."
—MICHAEL REDHILL, author of *Martin Sloane*

"*The Time in Between* is a spare, suspenseful meditation on the long reach of war—to the places where it is fought, the people who fight it, and the people who love those people. In portraying the lingering devastation left in one soldier's life by a war he fought a generation ago, Bergen's novel could not be timelier or more chilling."
—JENNIFER EGAN, author of *A Visit from the Goon Squad*

# STRANGER

# STRANGER

## DAVID BERGEN

THE OVERLOOK PRESS
NEW YORK, NY

First published in hardcover in the United States in 2017 by
The Overlook Press, Peter Mayer Publishers, Inc.

141 Wooster Street
New York, NY 10012
www.overlookpress.com
For bulk and special sales please contact sales@overlookny.com,
or write us at the above address.

Interior photos on pages VI–VII and 254–255 appear courtesy
of the photographer, Tom Waters.

Library of Congress Cataloging-in-Publication Data

Names: Bergen, David, 1957- author.
Title: Stranger / David Bergen.
Description: New York, NY : Overlook Press, 2017.
Identifiers: LCCN 2017002709 | ISBN 9781468315103 (hardcover)
Subjects: LCSH: Parental kidnapping--Fiction. | Single mothers--Fiction. |
Motherhood--Fiction. | Domestic fiction.
Classification: LCC PR9199.3.B413 S77 2017 | DDC 813/.54--dc23
LC record available at https://lccn.loc.gov/2017002709

Manufactured in the United States of America

ISBN: 978-1-4683-1510-3

1 3 5 7 9 10 8 6 4 2

*To Vicki and Tom*

# STRANGER

# I.

Rumour had it that the doctor's wife was coming to take the waters at Ixchel. The clinic was located in the highlands of Guatemala, at the edge of a lake that was eighty-four thousand years old. You came for the lake, and for the beauty of the three volcanoes, and for the quaintness of the twelve villages that surrounded the basin of the lake, and for the afternoon winds that were thought to carry away sin. But if you were a woman who was infertile, you came to take the waters.

Íso Perdido, who lived in the village and worked as a keeper at the clinic, had heard of the wife's imminent arrival. The doctor himself had told her. His wife was to arrive on Sunday. Even so, when Íso arrived at work on Monday morning and was given her assignment, she looked at the name on the card and wanted to say that she couldn't. But she had no good reason to give, or no reason that was safe. And so she prepared herself. She changed into wide black pants and a black top. She wore sandals. No jewellery and no makeup. She pulled her hair back in a ponytail with a hand-carved barrette. She went to the doctor's wife's room and knocked on the door. A voice called out and she entered.

She was at the table, finishing her breakfast. Her back, as she sat, was very erect and rigid. Her hair was blonde, like her husband's, but it was straighter, and it was shiny, as if it had been brushed and then brushed again. Her face was sharp and long, her eyes blue. She half rose from her seat and then sat down again.

Íso introduced herself. She said, I'll be your keeper for the next two weeks. If you need anything, simply ask. If you're unhappy, tell me. I'm here for you. Everyone at the clinic is here for you. We only want the best. She paused briefly and then asked, Should we begin, Mrs. Mann?

Please. Call me Susan, the doctor's wife said. And then she said that there were many expectations and she didn't know if she could live up to them.

This was a typical confession, immediate and without boundaries.

No expectations, Íso said. Only hope and goodwill.

The wife's face went soft.

Íso offered her a hand. She said that she would help her change.

Oh, I can manage.

Íso said that it was best to accept help. At first you might be shy. But you'll get used to me and soon it will feel normal.

Íso led her into the bedroom and took a robe from the closet. Rubber sandals. A towel. She laid all of this on the bed. The doctor's wife was wearing a white blouse with a Peter Pan collar, and it was fastened down the back. Íso began to unbutton the blouse. She slid it off, folded it, and laid it on a chair. She said that she would now remove Susan's bra. She did so and laid it on top of the blouse. She moved around to face the doctor's wife, whose hands fluttered up towards her chest and then back to her hips. Many of the women who came to the clinic were afraid of their bodies. A woman might walk around naked, but then avert her eyes when she passed by a mirror. Or she might carry herself as if curling into a cocoon. Or she might walk on tiptoes, as if the floor below might crack.

It's all right, Íso said. You're safe. She kneeled and released the wife's belt and undid her buttons and pulled down her jeans.

And your underwear, Íso said. She helped her.

The wife lifted one foot, then the other.

Íso saw the length of her neck, her jaw, the size of her breasts, her navel, the thin strip of pubic hair, her legs, the narrowness of her feet. Inevitably, she compared herself and she felt inferior, and this made her breathless and she thought that everything was impossible. But then she focused again and helped Susan into her robe. She tied it.

May I put your hair into a braid? she asked.

Susan nodded.

Íso wove a single thick braid. Susan's hair was very long and very beautiful, and Íso told her so.

I wonder sometimes if I'd cut it, and then I might get pregnant. My husband thinks this is nonsense.

Íso said that she didn't think anything was nonsense.

Do you know him? the wife asked.

Everyone knows Doctor Mann.

I haven't seen him yet. Everything is strange. The vegetation, the waves against the shore, the men who fish at night outside my bedroom window. She said she'd heard a knocking and thought that someone wanted to enter, but it was only oars banging against the gunnels of a boat. Coming in by car yesterday she'd seen a little boy carrying a huge bundle of sticks on his back. Like an image from the underworld, she said. My husband told me not to get my hopes up. What do you think?

Íso said that hope was never harmful. In any case, there were no rules.

She said that it was time, and she led her outside and down a cobbled path, beneath the jacaranda trees, and into the pool area, which was surrounded by walls of bamboo. She told Susan that she would take the waters twice a day. In the morning and in the afternoon. After each bath she would receive a massage that would focus on her womb.

At the pool's edge, Íso reached to untie Susan's robe.

Could I wear a bathing suit? Susan asked.

It's better to let the water touch you everywhere, Íso said. Don't worry, we're alone.

They were. The pool was not large, and it was heated, and above them there were skylights. Íso wore her pants and top. She stepped down into the pool with Susan. Susan floated naked on her back as Íso supported her. There was music playing softly. Íso, as she did with other patients, tried to look elsewhere, and not at the body she was holding. But she was aware of how slight Susan was, and she was aware of Susan's face and its vulnerability, and of how Susan closed her eyes and turned away as if to hide. Íso thought of the doctor's hands touching the body she was now holding. It was too much, and so she thought of English verbs and irregular conjugations.

As they came up the stairs from the pool, Íso retrieved the robe and held it open for Susan and then tied it in front. She felt Susan's breath on the crown of her head as she bowed. They crossed the cobbled path and descended a small staircase into a cave-like room with an oval skylight. The room held a shower, a steam bath, and a narrow bed. Íso excused herself and changed into a dark blue sleeveless shift that came to just below her knees. It made her look androgynous. She returned to the room where Susan waited.

In the shower Susan sat on the chair and Íso released her hair from its braid and it fell to the small of her back. Íso soaked Susan's hair and took some shampoo and lathered her scalp. Her forehead was broad and her skin was smooth and almost translucent. Íso could see the small blue veins, like many lines drawn by a thin pencil.

It's a workout, washing my hair, Susan said.

It's beautiful, Íso said.

If I don't succeed this time, off it goes, Susan said.

Íso was quiet.

I've been trying for three years, Susan said. It's a strange thing, but I have to continually fight against the shame. Why shame? I haven't done anything wrong. I haven't acted badly. But I still feel shame.

Íso had heard all this before, from many other women. The shame. But she'd never heard it from someone so intimately connected to her. She rinsed Susan's hair and twisted the water from it and the water ran down Susan's back. She asked Susan to stand, and then she turned on the shower and soaped her body. Her breasts, her stomach, and between her legs. There were women who did not want Íso to wash between their legs, but Susan, for all her shyness, did not mind, nor did she balk at having her pubis massaged. It was considered an important part of the treatment, as the massaging might stimulate fertility.

Susan was limber, and she had a genuine pelvis with a shallow cavity, which meant less trauma when giving birth. Íso thought that she would tell Susan later in the week, when she might need encouragement.

She kneeled and washed Susan's calves and ankles and feet. She asked her to lift one foot at a time. Susan did so, leaning forward with her palms against the shower wall. Íso took an emery board and kneeled and worked at Susan's heels, though she did not have calluses. Her feet were white and clean and smooth, like polished enamel.

After, she asked Susan to lie down on the bed. She laid towels over Susan's chest and her legs, and she massaged her stomach. Susan was now completely silent. The only sound was of Íso's hands, like paper shuffling, on Susan's body.

Susan began to cry. She wept without noise, and the tears dropped onto the sheets. Íso kept touching her, massaging her uterus and her bowels, cresting near the ribcage, and then descending towards the pubis. And then Susan was laughing softly, and she looked at Íso and said, Oh my, that's never happened before.

Later, Íso gave Susan drops of Vitex agnus-castus and two pills of bovine colostrum. Then she handed Susan her robe and led her back to her room.

Sometimes a patient would leave a small tip for Íso, but on this day Susan did not give her anything. Íso, because she never expected a tip, was not surprised. Susan, like most of the women, had her mind on other things.

In the afternoon, Íso found Susan in her room and took her temperature. When she was finished Susan asked if she had ever witnessed a case where a woman became pregnant.

It can happen, Íso said.

And it had happened, several times, though the role the clinic played in the pregnancy was always unclear. But the clinic liked success stories, for they encouraged more women to come and take the waters.

Susan asked about her husband. Have you seen him? she asked.

Íso was quiet for a moment, and then she said, Here, at the clinic?

Yes, here.

He's working today.

When I called and told him I was coming, he wasn't pleased. I insisted. He won't see me the first week, which is superstitious, don't you think?

Those are the procedures here, Íso said. You're supposed to focus on yourself.

It's just odd, to imagine him so close. My skin is very aware.

That's important, Íso said. It's good for your body.

A year ago, when we learned that we couldn't get pregnant, we stopped having sex, Susan said.

Íso had no words.

He might have been interested. As an act. But I wasn't. What's the point? She was quiet for a long time and then spoke very softly, as if fearful that someone other than Íso might hear. She said that she had gone to find other men, maybe to hurt her husband, maybe out of sadness, but certainly to find out the truth. She didn't get pregnant. And she was sorry that she had embarrassed herself in various ways.

She didn't explain what the various ways were, and Íso didn't ask. She led Susan to the pool to take the waters once again, and then she showered her, and once again she massaged her, but this time there were no tears. All was silent save for the birds that sang wildly in the trees outside. And the El Norte that blew in off the lake.


Íso had worked at the clinic for two years. When she finished high school, she'd lived in the city and gone to university in preparation for medicine, but her school funds were soon depleted and she'd returned to her village to work with the women at the clinic, who were most often foreigners. She had learned that desperation in a woman's face and body was not a pretty sight. Desperation and sadness and false happiness and hope and wishful thinking and physical ache—all of this was mixed up and thrown into a tempest, and what survived, what fell to the earth, was disappointment.

Íso's view of the world was limited to her own needs and her own passions and to the needs and passions of her family and small circle of friends. She felt for the women who arrived at the clinic so full of hope. But when they were gone, she forgot about them.

The clinic had come about by a series of contingencies. An American scientist, Doctor August, had visited the lake six years earlier with his wife, who was thought to be infertile. His wife bathed in the waters of the lake and underwent a series of local procedures (the baths, the massages, the ingestion of aguacolla, the smoking of the roots and bulbs of the water lily), and she became pregnant. After his wife gave birth to a healthy boy, the scientist claimed that the waters of the lake were responsible, and he built the clinic, to which women came, full of optimism. And the women went home confident. And failed to become pregnant. But this disappointment did not halt their return. Some women had come back three or four times.

Believing that one's surroundings were essential to constructive thoughts and positive results, Doctor August set up birthing chambers in the clinic. At the entrance to each chamber, carved into the lintel, was an image of Ixchel, the Mayan goddess of creation and destruction. These chambers were offered to the local women free of charge. Nurses and doctors and midwives were present. And so, the giving of birth was paired with the treatment for infertility, and the hope was that the former would affect the latter. But it only made the infertile women sadder. What could be worse than wishing very much for a child, and observing through a one-way mirror the birth of a stranger's child, and hearing the cries of a stranger's newborn?

The job of a keeper, the most important aspect, was to be both present and invisible. Doctor August had invented a name for this. Igual. Physically, it was like floating, and eventually the patient came to accept that the keeper would always be present, but that the presence was never invasive. The keeper became an object, much like a remote control or a timepiece. The perfect keeper would always be available.

Íso depended on igual as she worked with the doctor's wife. For nine hours every day, she floated in that space where her own existence was nothing. And then she walked through the village back to her mother's tienda, and it was during these walks that she let go of the weight of the women she served, and their unhappiness, which was not her unhappiness. Sometimes, when they worked the same shift, she and Illya walked together to the playa, where Illya would catch a boat back to Panajachel, and as they walked they laughed and gossiped about the women they worked with. Illya was working with a British woman who kept correcting Illya's English. I *khant*, Illya said, I *khant*. And she said that the English woman, Mrs. Hadley, had had an orgasm during her massage. Yes, she *khan*, Illya said. She laughed and wrapped her arm around Íso's shoulder.

Typically, when Íso arrived home, she ate supper with her mother, and then she sat at the counter in the tienda and she tended to the customers and she worked at her reading for the literature course she took every Saturday morning at the American School in Panajachel. Her mother appeared now and then in the dimness of the tienda, but by 9 p.m. she had disappeared and found her bed. Íso would join her around eleven, and she would read for fifteen minutes, and then she would turn out the light and fall asleep, and at some point during the night her mother would be holding Íso's hip, or perhaps clutching her hand, and then Íso would fall asleep again, and sometimes she would dream and in the dreams she was often in charge of a young child, or a frail woman who resembled a child, and she had a difficult time keeping track of her charge. This particular dream always left her with a sense of foreboding. In the morning, she rose, had a light breakfast of papaya and coffee, and returned to the clinic.

SHE hadn't seen Doctor Mann all that week. He'd been deliberately absent, or he'd avoided her, or she'd avoided him. And then he phoned her Friday evening, and she felt the same way she always did when she saw him after an absence, or when she heard his voice on the phone—a closing of the throat, a little leap in her chest, a fire in her brain, a blood vessel beating behind her right eye.

He asked how she was, and she said she was fine. He said the week had been long, and she said, Forever. He said, She adores you, and to this she had no answer. The desire she'd felt upon first hearing his voice had left her.

I haven't spoken with her, he said, but others, they've heard. You've won her heart.

Why are you telling me this? she said. I don't want to know who she loves and why. *Your* heart. That's what I want. Not hers. I miss you terribly. When I'm working with her, when she speaks, when I think of the two of you, I miss you.

Yes, he said. I know. I know.

For a moment she imagined that Eric was a weak man who wanted everything for no price. She was confused. She felt unsafe and vulnerable. Does she know about us? she asked.

Nothing. She suspects nothing.

But she should know.

This isn't the time.

Then I will tell her.

You could. But it wouldn't change anything. She means nothing to me. You mean everything.

She was quiet. Then she said, She's like all the other women I've treated. She's spoiled. She's sad. She's full of want. She's greedy. She sees only herself.

You're angry.

No. I'm only telling the truth. Then she said that she didn't want to think about the next day.

It's nothing, he said.

To me it is everything. And to her it is everything. Do you want a child with her?

No, I don't.

Then why have sex with her?

I won't.

Of course you will. What else will you do? Play checkers? She tells me that her skin is aware of your presence. She's been waiting. Íso began to cry. And as she cried silently, holding the phone to her ear, she was ashamed to reveal herself in this way.

He said her name, over and over, and when she was able to speak again, she said that she was going dancing with Illya on Saturday night, in Pana. You could come with me, she said.

I could.

But you won't.

Íso.

It makes me sad.

Don't be. One more week.

Say that you love me.

And so he said that he loved her, and then she said that she loved him, but after he had hung up her chest ached, and she thought that she might be a fool to imagine she had any advantage over a woman like Susan.

On Saturday, riding the boat to Panajachel, she was aware of the day and what it meant. The waves were high and the bow of the boat rose and fell and the hull banged steadily and the banging sound was full of meaning, as were the wind and the spray that hit her face. After class, at 1 p.m., as she walked over to visit Illya, she was aware that Eric would be meeting his wife for tea, and she knew that they would be going out for dinner that evening. And she knew that they would have sex. Husbands often visited their wives at the clinic during the second week of treatment, when the patient was more relaxed and open. Open. The word was full of meaning.

Íso had known Illya for many years—they had graduated together. Illya's mother was from Argentina and her father was from Spain, and they owned a shop in Panajachel that sold copper cooking pots shipped in from France. The mother, Rosa, was in fact the one with the business head, and she ran the shop while the father, Eduardo, sat at home and smoked up and organized the books for the business in his disorganized manner. Illya loved her father, because he made no demands on her.

Illya knew about Doctor Mann. Right from the beginning, after the doctor's first visit to the tienda, Íso had told her everything.

Illya had asked what would happen when the doctor went back to the States.

We'll still be friends, Íso said.

You'd be lucky to catch him, Illya said.

He'd be lucky to catch me.

Is he a playboy? Illya asked.

No. No.

Maybe he'll invite you to his home, Illya said. Come with me. Be my lover.

What would I do in the States? I don't even have permission

papers. In any case, the border is sealed. He doesn't talk like that.

Illya took Íso's head in her hands and kissed her on the forehead. Be careful, she said. Men can be greedy. Does he speak Spanish with you?

English.

Spanish is more romantic, Illya said.

Eric's Spanish is not romantic. It's elementary. Everything's in the present.

That's the problem. Teach him the future tense.

And they had laughed.

Today, she found Illya in the garden with her boxer, Bella. Illya came to her and kissed her and took her arm and they sat side by side while Bella panted at their feet.

Íso said, He's with his wife right now.

Illya made a face. She said, Susan Mann has no advantage over you. She's desperate. She's hanging on. We've both seen her kind before. A skinny gringa. You have to be colder. Then he will come to you. The more you pull, she said, the more he'll run. A boy, a man, he is like an untrained dog who thinks that because you don't allow him to sniff the pole over there, that pole is the most precious spot in the world. Let him go, she said. And he will come running back.

She bent to kiss Bella's head. You beautiful bitch, she said.

They washed each other's hair that afternoon, and then tried on dresses and skirts and tops, finally choosing something that Illya said was sexy. She said that to find another man would make the doctor jealous. Íso said she had no interest in other men.

That evening they went to a club and danced together, and Íso ignored the boys and the men. She loved the music, the bass as it moved through her body, the sweating, Illya across from her, eyes closed, her small body swaying. They left the club late and walked back to Illya's house and ate cold watermelon in the garden alongside the kitchen. They talked about the boys at the club, and they talked about men in general, and then they talked about love, and Illya spoke of her fiancé in Argentina, and of her upcoming marriage. And so, for a time, Íso forgot about the doctor and his wife, and she forgot about her life on the other side of the lake.

On Monday, when she arrived at Doctor Mann's wife's door, she had prepared herself for tales of passion and desire, but Susan said nothing about Saturday. And because of this, it was clear that Eric had not spoken to her about Íso or about anything else that was important. Íso felt hollow. Her breathing was shallow and quick. Susan stood and began to remove her clothes in order to take the waters. She'd become very free in front of Íso. She stood naked before the mirror, inspecting herself. She asked if Íso liked her.

Yes, I do, Íso said.

I mean my body. Is it attractive?

Yes, it is, Íso said. She was looking at the back of Susan's head. She saw her hair and her one ear, and she saw Susan studying herself.

Susan said, A lover once told me that he liked my feet the best.

You have very beautiful feet.

They stepped into the pool.

Susan lay back and looked up at the grass roof. She closed her eyes. She said she was afraid that she would fail. That the rituals, the baths, the massages would not change her world. She said she missed having her period. She thought that men, even though they wouldn't admit it, were drawn to the blood.

Íso let her talk. She half listened. She was curious about the lover. She supposed that Susan might be right about the blood. The water was warm. She felt loose. Wild. In seven days she would be with him. They would ride his motorcycle into the highlands and halt by the side of the road and stand in the shade of a eucalyptus and hold each other. Later, in the evening, in his room, he would lie beside her while candles guttered on the dresser.

Susan opened her eyes. You're still here, she said. I couldn't feel you.

I'm here, Íso said.


THERE were three birthing chambers at the clinic. The chambers were cone-shaped and the cone sat on its head so that the widest part opened to the skylight above. Observation rooms sat above the chamber, and during a birth these rooms were occupied by the women who had come to the clinic to take the waters in the hopes of curing their infertility. On Tuesday afternoon, Íso and Susan watched the birth of a child who was to be "handed over," a process arranged by the clinic. The birth mother was a young woman, in her early twenties. There was a nurse present, and a local midwife. The mother-to-be was lying on the bed. She was very quiet, even when the contractions arrived. She did not ask for help. She did not want medication. She breathed quickly and turned her head to the side, and then she raised her head from the pillow on the bed and she bent forward as if to discover something far below her, and the baby was born. How surely and efficiently it all happened. The midwife caught the baby. She cut the umbilical cord. She wrapped the baby in a blanket. She smoothed the baby's head. Kissed it. And then the baby was passed to the mother. The mother held it at a distance. She touched the hands and then the feet. Released the blanket and inspected the infant thoroughly. A door into the chamber opened and an older woman appeared. She was dressed in white. She approached and held out her hands for the baby, and the mother passed the infant into the older woman's arms. The woman in white then turned and left the chamber. The young mother lay down and eventually produced the afterbirth. Her face was without passion. Again, she did not cry out.

The doctor's wife seemed overwhelmed. That's all? she said. She doesn't get to hold the baby? To breastfeed?

No. It's too difficult. She'll never see the child again.

She asked if Íso ever got used to watching.

Íso didn't respond directly. She said that a woman never gave up two babies. It was too difficult. Even though the demand was high and the price good.

The baby was beautiful, said Susan.

Íso agreed. She said that the child was very healthy.

The doctor's wife was holding Íso's hand. As if a friend. Íso was aware of Susan's shallow breaths, and of the clenching and unclenching of Susan's fingers against her own hand. She was so lost. Íso felt her own heart grow cold.

And her heart grew even colder the following day. Susan lay naked on the massage bed, face down, her bottom covered by a towel. She asked Íso if she had children of her own.

Íso said that she didn't.

Susan asked if she would like to have children.

I think someday, Íso said.

Susan spoke of the infant who had been taken the day before. It was sad to watch, but the child would have tremendous advantages. Money, food, comfort, education, citizenship, freedom.

All those things are available here, Íso said. Immediately she was sorry. It was not her place to argue with a patient, even if the patient was wrong.

Of course, Susan said. You're right. But you're mistaken as well. What we have in America is a surplus. It doesn't make us better—that's just the way it is.

Íso helped the doctor's wife turn onto her back. She covered Susan's breasts and her crotch with warm towels. Her ribcage was sharply defined. Her concave stomach, her belly button. Íso felt appalled by Susan's emptiness, her vanity, her ignorance. Her hands were shaking, and she worried that Susan would notice. And so she descended into igual. She wished for nothing.

The week passed.

Susan said goodbye to Íso on Friday afternoon. She would depart the following morning, early. Íso was surprised by Susan's warmth, and her generous hug, and the looseness in her body.

Think of me, Susan said.

I will, Íso answered.

Susan kissed her on one cheek and then the other. She clasped Íso's hands. She hugged her again.

I'm afraid, Susan said.

I know, Íso said.

I may return.

It's possible.

And you will be here.

That's probable.

Susan laughed.

Íso stepped back.

And they parted.

# 2.

DOCTOR ERIC MANN HAD ARRIVED AT THE CLINIC IN JANUARY, in the midst of the dry season, six months before the appearance of his wife. He was an American gynaecologist who was attractive and elegant and friendly. He was very popular: with the director, who was happy to have an American doctor at the clinic; with the keepers, who found him to be both handsome and carefree; and with the patients themselves, who claimed that the doctor's hands had mysterious powers. Rumour had it that Doctor Eric Mann had been married, but that his wife had left him and so he was now single. What was exactly true was unclear. He lived off the clinic grounds, at a hotel that bordered the lake, and he was frequently seen on weekends riding his motorcycle to the various pueblos that surrounded the lake. He was quite a sight, with his long blond hair flowing out behind him and his sunglasses.

The picture he presented was romantic and tender, almost to the point of caricature. His attempts at speaking the local language endeared him to the people. He might have thought of himself as an American Che, a doctor who worked with the poor and lowly, only he worked mostly with the wealthy and despondent women who appeared at the clinic. Women who no longer loved themselves, but hoped to rekindle that love as they took the waters. In truth, Doctor Mann was interested in the people from the village. He had greater affection for them than he did for the wealthy women he treated. He proposed to the director that the clinic should be expanded to include general care for the villagers: physicals, treatments of infections, minor outpatient surgery, dietary guidance, maternity advice. And so it came to be that these services were provided, and were funded by the thousands of dollars that the barren women paid to take the waters.

The first time Íso spoke to Doctor Mann it was as a translator for a village girl who was five months pregnant and was spotting. The girl was very young, about seventeen, and though it was not uncommon in the region for girls that young to have children, the doctor seemed surprised by her youthfulness. If the girl felt pain, she did not show it. She and Íso spoke in the local dialect. Íso asked various questions. The girl explained that she had been in the hills with her husband, collecting firewood, and she had fainted.

Íso translated.

Doctor Mann asked if the girl had carried to full term before. Does she have other children?

Yes, Íso said. This is her second. Her first child is two. She had a miscarriage a year ago. Very similar to this. She began to spot, and then there was heavy bleeding and she lost the fetus.

And how do you know all this? Doctor Mann asked.

I asked. She told me. When Íso spoke she looked briefly into the doctor's face and his eyes, and then turned away slightly, in order to pay him respect. He was, after all, a doctor.

She's very young, Doctor Mann said. He recommended bedrest. She was to stay at the clinic.

The family can't afford it, Íso said.

She doesn't have to pay. She'll lose the baby if she goes home.

The husband will insist on taking her home.

That's silly. There is no understanding here of health or safety. It's all instinct and witchcraft. They're afraid of science.

Perhaps they're afraid because science doesn't have a heart or a soul.

Doctor Mann looked at her for a long time and then asked, What's your name?

She said that she was called "Eee-so." She spelled it: Í-S-O. She said that sometimes patients called her "eye-so." You're free to do that, of course, but I might not come when you call. She knew that she was being cheeky, but she couldn't help herself. She was nervous.

He said he hadn't heard that name before.

She said it was short for Paraíso.

He tried out her name, Paraíso, but the vowels were all wrong.

Íso is simplest, she said.

Of course.

And you're Doctor Mann, she said. Her statement appeared to be a mock greeting, but it wasn't. It was the first time she had addressed him directly, and because English didn't allow for the formal voice, she was off balance. She was also a little in awe, and still nervous, and when this happened, she tended to be dismissive. She knew of him. All the keepers were aware of him. They gossiped. They observed. They gossiped some more. Doctor Mann was impossible to miss as he strode through the corridors and gardens of the clinic.

Íso and the doctor were standing at the foot of the girl's bed. He was wearing his lab coat. The sleeves of the coat were too short and Íso noticed his wrists and the blond hair there. His fingers were slender. His stethoscope hung to the middle of his chest. His eyes were green or blue, and only later did she realize that they were like the waters of the lake, which shifted in moods from dark blue to green to light blue. At that time, at that moment, she didn't imagine that he had even noticed her, except as a translator. She had no designs. She was simply observing.

The doctor said that if the girl wanted to save the baby, she had to stay in bed. Even so, she might lose it.

Íso translated.

The girl nodded.

She asked the girl if she had someone to help her with the older child.

The girl said that her abuelita lived with them.

Good, Íso said.

She turned to explain this to the doctor, but he was gone.

~~~

A WEEK after Íso had translated for Doctor Mann, he stopped her on the path that wound down to the pool area and inquired about the girl. Was there news? Íso said she hadn't heard, but she could drop by the family's home and check on the girl. She knew the house.

In the evening, around dinnertime, Íso made her way to the home of the girl. The sun had set. The houses were lit. Young boys walked hand in hand in the streets, and a child squatted near the entrance to her family's tienda. Nearby, an old woman sat before her fruit press, her clean glasses stacked beside the basket of oranges. Íso greeted everyone she met, and they greeted her in return.

The house of the pregnant girl was built from cinder blocks, the roof was corrugated metal, the floor was packed earth upon which there were scattered various rugs of bright colours. The girl was lying on a bed in the front room. Her abuela sat beside the bed. Íso was offered tea. She declined. She stood before the girl and asked if all was fine.

The girl nodded.

No more blood? Íso asked.

The girl said that she had not bled since leaving the clinic.

Íso asked if the baby had been moving at all.

The girl nodded.

Like before?

Yes, the girl said. The baby is very strong.

The abuela listened and nodded. She held the older child in her lap.

I'd like to look, Íso said. Okay?

The girl said that she could look.

Íso lifted the girl's T-shirt and touched her abdomen. She pressed against the wall of the uterus and asked if there was any pain. Here? And here? There?

Each time the girl shook her head.

And you're staying in bed as the doctor said?

Yes.

She told the girl that she wanted to see if there was blood. Okay? The girl agreed. Íso slipped the girl's underwear down to her thighs. She saw no fresh blood. She pulled up the girl's underwear and replaced the blanket. She smiled. It was much easier to work with a Tz'utujil woman than with the foreigners at the clinic. She stood and said that Doctor Mann had asked after the girl. He was concerned. She said that if there was any problem—if there was more blood, or if the girl fainted or felt weak, or if she noticed that the baby was not moving—she should come back to the clinic. Okay?

The girl nodded.

The abuela spoke. She said that she herself had had six children, all girls. And she'd had two children who were born dead, and these two were both boys. She said that a child knows if it's healthy. And if this is so, it will come into the world. Otherwise, it won't. She said that her granddaughter's baby would be born in twelve weeks, and it would be a boy. She took Íso's hand and thanked her.

The following day, Íso told Doctor Mann that the girl was fine. She said that the abuela knew everything there was to know about childbirth, and she even knew the sex of the baby. The pregnant mother was in good hands.

Doctor Mann said that every grandmother in the village believed she was a midwife, or a doctor, or a soothsayer, and that had proven to be a problem in the past. They don't know about malpresentation, he said. They don't understand preeclampsia.

Not the words, Íso said, but they know the physical problem. They are women. They've had babies before.

He studied her. He asked her age.

She said she was twenty-two.

He said, You seem older.

This was obviously flirtatious, almost wrong, but she didn't care, and it surprised her that she didn't care. He asked where she had learned to speak English without an accent. She said at the American School in Panajachel. He asked about her intentions. Did she plan to stay at the clinic, working as a keeper? She said that once she had enough money, she planned to go to the city and continue studying medicine. Her goal was to graduate and then work at a local hospital. She wondered, when she said this, if he might think that she was making this up on the spot, or that she was only trying to impress him, to match him in some way. But it was true, medicine was her intention. And it was the dream of her mother, who had spent much of the money she had made from the tienda on sending Íso across the lake to the American School. She was an only child. There were hopes and expectations.

~~~~~

WHEN Doctor Mann arrived one day at the door to her mother's tienda, it appeared to be by chance, but it wasn't. He'd come looking for her. He bought a quart of ice cream and ate it as he stood beneath the awning of the shop. It was a Sunday, his day off, and her day off as well. They spoke English. He told her that her English was very smooth and pure. This is how he put it. Pure. He was flattering and clear and kind, and he looked her in the eyes as he spoke these words, and because he wasn't a doctor at that moment and she wasn't a keeper, she looked at his eyes and saw that they were blue.

He offered her some ice cream, but she refused because it hurt her teeth. He said that she should call him Eric. The other makes me feel old, he said.

She asked his age.

He said he was thirty. Is that old? he asked.

She said it didn't matter to her.

You're a strange one, he said. And then he said he would see her again, and he climbed on his motorcycle and left her standing in the street. She sat behind the counter in the tienda and tried not to think of him, but this was impossible. And so she thought about the colour of his hair and the colour of his eyes and the slight crookedness of his mouth that made it seem as if he was just about to smile, and the manner in which he leaned into her as he asked her questions, as if no one else existed save her. Even later, when they became very close, and when they were out with a group of interns or other foreigners, she was aware of how explicit he was in his attention to the person he was speaking with. It didn't have to be her. Though she wanted it to be. And she suffered jealousy, a feeling she had never experienced in a large way before. The jealousy surprised her. She felt unbalanced, and she wondered where such a strong emotion had come from.

In the evenings he began to drop by the tienda, where she sat behind the counter serving customers and, when there was a lull, reading and writing. She was always waiting, listening for the sound of his motorcycle—the low, smooth hum of the Honda, which was cleaner and softer than the tinny racket of the Chinese-made motorcycles that moved up the street towards the market. He approached from the playa, following the one-way street, and he parked his bike, turned it off, and pushed back his blond hair. He swung his leg over the saddle and walked into the tienda and said good evening to her in Spanish. She pretended surprise, even though she had been watching him, and she responded in Spanish and for a time they spoke her language, and when his restricted vocabulary was depleted, they spoke English. He was very good at not talking about himself, even though she wanted to hear about his life. He asked her what she was reading and she told him, and he asked about her Saturdays at the American School and she told him that she was taking a class in English literature, and he asked her if she was smart, and she laughed and said she was all right.

I think so, he said. He asked about her friends and she told him about Illya, who also worked as a keeper. You must know her, she said.

He did.

She said that Illya was her best friend. She held her hand to her chest when she said this, surprising herself with the emotion she felt.

He asked if there was a boy who was also such a good friend, a novio, and she said, Sin novio. She asked him if there was a novia in his life.

He said no.

No wife? she asked. This was very forward, but she wanted to know. In fact, she thought that if he was going to flirt with her, she had the right to know.

No more, he said.

What does that mean? she asked. She's dead?

He laughed. No, I live here and she lives there. We're separated.

Íso nodded. And this is true? she asked. She said that her mother would like to know.

True, he said. You can tell your mother. Are there any other questions?

She tilted her head. What's her name? she asked.

Susan.

Is she beautiful?

In her way.

What way is that?

As someone who is aware that others are looking at her.

He might just as easily have been describing himself, but she did not share this thought. She kept it as part of her tally, in which she gauged who he was and how he behaved, and how he might reveal himself to her. This was still early on, when she was capable of some objectivity, before she tumbled into adoration.

Sometimes, on those evenings when he called on her, her mother appeared, and then he did what he did best. He paid attention to Señora Perdido, whom he had met during one of his first visits. He looked right at Señora Perdido and said it was a pleasure, and then he asked her if she was happy with her smart daughter who was strong and beautiful, and of course Señora Perdido nodded her head and said yes, yes. Another time he praised the store, saying that it was stocked with things foreigners wanted, and this was a good thing. The first time he met Señora Perdido he said that she could easily be Íso's sister, and this was true to a point, for she was still young and her face was youthful. Señora Perdido bowed her head. He made little flourishes as he spoke, and Íso was aware of his hands. When he addressed Señora Perdido, his vocabulary was weak, and sometimes they spoke English, a language in which Señora Perdido was quite adept. But the content of his speech was of little matter. It was the presentation, the company of this young man, that impressed Señora Perdido. And she was won over. In those moments.

Íso did not tell anyone, and she might have denied the truth even to herself, though when he was near, when she smelled him, when she heard him speak, even when he was talking to someone else, she understood. Love was supposed to be complex and without a solution, or so she thought until she suffered it, and then she saw that it had no conditions, and that it was simple and brimming. Her heart ached. And her shoulders and her breasts and her thighs.

There'd been one other before him, a boy from her village who used to ride the boat to school with her, and with whom she'd read assignments, and to whom she'd offered the occasional kiss in a dark street near the market, leaning against the stone wall of a carpintería, folding into each other so that she and he were one. But now she realized that boy had been nothing. Nothing.

Doctor Mann had the motorcycle, and within a month they were riding together on Sundays to the various pueblos around the lake or down to Patulul, where they walked through the market. He would pick her up early, and because he had only one helmet he insisted she wear it and so she did. The wind blew his hair back against the shield of her helmet, and she wrapped her arms around his waist, and when the road was straight, he took his left hand and held her wrist or her fingers. And then, after returning to the pueblo, he parked the motorcycle beside his bungalow, which was behind the hotel that overlooked the lake. They sat on his porch, he in the hammock, she in a chair, and he drank a Gallo while she drank water. And they talked. She said that she loved this time in the evening, when the birds had settled down, and the day was over, and the tumult of the day had finished. She chose the word "tumult" because he had used it just that morning when talking about the tumult of his heart. She liked the word but thought that it was much too dramatic to talk about his heart. It was too intimate.

He said that she was hard to reach.

I'm not, she said. I'm right here.

She had not thought about him physically, other than in a dreamy way, and in her inexperience she imagined lying with him in a clean bed, side by side, fully clothed, and they held hands and talked, and perhaps kissed, but they did not touch other than to stroke each other's face, and they spoke of love but did not act on it. And so it had to be that the first time she acted on her love for him, she was utterly surprised by his quick, hard need. She was also surprised by the colour of his body. She of course knew that he was blond and his hands were white and his face was white, but she was not prepared for his whole body to be white, and for a moment, when he stood before her, everything was a surprise. She kept her T-shirt and socks on, which made her feel safer, and yet unclean in some way, and when he slid her T-shirt up to her neck and kissed her there, she thought this was all fair and good, but it was not as she had imagined it. There was some tenderness, and he called her beautiful, but it was as if he was talking to himself. The lamp beside his bed was on, and though it was dim, she asked if it might be turned off. He did so. And then it was dark, and it was easier, because now his body was in the shadows, and she could have him without actually seeing him, and she found it good to touch him and be touched. She felt his breath on her neck and on her cheeks and on the top of her head, and she imagined a white piece of paper on which there was nothing, and all that nothingness turned into layers of clouds through which she fell. When it was over, she thought, So this is it.

She became freer. They sometimes went to his room in the afternoons, occasionally on Saturdays, when he met her by the pier as she returned from school in Panajachel. On those days, she hopped on the back of his bike and they rode straight to his bungalow. She had become accustomed to being with him in the afternoon light. She liked to study his body. And she liked him to touch and talk to her body. At times they were careless, or lazy, and didn't use a condom. She wondered later, when she was alone, if she wanted something that she wasn't even aware of.

ONE Sunday he invited her to ride down the coast with him to Tecojate. A few of the doctors were going there for the day, to swim and eat lunch and enjoy the water. She said that she didn't know how to swim. He said that it wasn't necessary. He wanted her there. She agreed, and so they rode down through San Lucas Tolimán and past the large fincas into the heat of Patulul and towards the coast. She had been to Tecojate only once, as a child, and she discovered that it had not changed. You parked and walked over to the river and crossed the river on a small boat, which cost five quetzales for a round trip, and then you walked past a few tiendas and settled into one of the comedores. The ocean with its large waves was one hundred yards beyond, and on Sundays it was full of those who were seeking reprieve from the heat. Three other doctors who worked at the clinic rode up by van and joined them. Hanna was from Germany, and Hans and Betje, a married couple, were from Holland. Íso had met all three doctors at the clinic, and so she knew them and they knew her, but they paid little attention to her, just as they did at the clinic, other than to ask about her plans and her mother, and so it turned out that the questions were always the same, and the answers the same as well, and soon they ran out of things to say. She would have been pleased to have a larger conversation, but it wasn't her place to ask them questions.

And of course, there was the issue of bathing suits. Hanna and Betje wore bikinis, and though this didn't bother Íso, she was aware of her own modesty, of the shorts and large T-shirt she had changed into. This was her swimming outfit—it was what she and her friends had always worn at the beach, though Illya, being Illya, wore a bikini when swimming. When they all walked down to the beach Íso was aware of Hanna and Betje's beauty, and their freedom with their bodies, and of her own attire, especially when she got wet and the T-shirt clung to her skin. She kept pulling at her T-shirt in order to hide her shape, but no one seemed to notice, and so she gave up and walked out into the waves with Eric and when a large wave crashed over them, she gasped and Eric took her hand. She pushed him out into the surf. Go, she said, and he did, diving into the waves, following the others, and she went back to the shore and watched them catch the large waves, their arms and bodies and hair all the same colour, except for Hanna, whose hair was dark and long. And then Hanna was sitting on Eric's shoulders and she was laughing, her head thrown back, and her body was shining in the sun. Íso walked back through the hot sand and lay in a hammock beneath the roof of the comedor, and she closed her eyes, and she must have slept, because she now heard Hanna talking, and she opened her eyes and saw that the four doctors were sitting at the table, and they were smoking a joint. Eric saw that she was awake, and he said, Come, join us. And so she did, and Eric offered her the joint, but she shook her head no.

Hanna was talking about the women in the village. She said it was an utter tragedy. They wanted to have their tubes tied, but they needed the signature of the husband, which rarely happened, and even when they did get the signature, the father would intervene and say no. She said the other day she'd done a C-section and tied the woman's tubes without the husband or father knowing. The girl had requested it, whispered in Hanna's ear before she went under. Nineteen years old, Hanna said, and already a mother of three.

Betje said that the women in the villages amazed her. So solid. So capable. Yet trapped beneath this rock of patriarchy. And then the husband runs off and takes a lover and spends all his money on his mistress. She said that it was absurd to tie a woman's tubes in a fertility clinic.

Íso listened. She was worried that they would ask her opinion on some matter relating to men or women and children, or something about men and power, but no one asked her for her thoughts. She was relieved. They talked as if everything was clear and certain.

Eric was quiet.

For lunch they ate a mixto of shrimp and fish and they drank beer. She drank water and ate delicately, aware of how Hanna tore at her shrimp, her fingers dripping with sauce.

God, Hanna said, I feel like a pig.

You are a pig, Hans said, and he wiped at her face with a napkin. Betje was stooped over her fish, picking at the bones. She seemed very stoned. And for a moment Íso wished that she were freer for Eric's sake. She wished that she could smoke dope and wear a bikini and drink beer with abandon, and then perhaps he would find her more attractive.

After lunch, Hans, Betje, and Hanna went for another swim. Íso and Eric watched them run into the waves.

Hanna's beautiful, Íso said.

Eric shrugged. She talks too much, he said. She knows everything.

If you know everything, then you're allowed to talk.

She *thinks* she knows everything.

And you?

He turned to look at her. Me?

Do you know everything?

Nothing. I know nothing. Especially about you.

My mother says I'm still young. She's worried. Do you wish I had a bikini?

Do you want one? Your body's perfect. You have nothing to be ashamed of.

I'm not ashamed. And then she said, You should have an American girlfriend, or a German girlfriend.

Why?

Because they're free.

They might look free, but they aren't. Believe me. You're free.

How am I free?

You're free to be modest. You're free to not smoke up. You're free to be here and listen and not respond to the nonsense that Hanna spouts. You're very calm, and you're very comfortable with yourself.

I'm insignificant to them, she said, and she waved her hand in the direction of the three doctors.

Next time we'll come alone, he said.

But you like them, she said.

I put up with them.

She said that she found them funny. You come here and think you know about us. You talk about men and patriarchy and tubes tied. And you talk about poverty. You don't know half of it.

You? he asked. You're including me? He took her hand and held it.

Not you, she said.

On the return trip they stopped at a dairy finca, on the outskirts of San Lucas, where there was a very modern shop that sold ice cream. They stood beside the motorcycle and ate ice cream cones. She had removed her helmet and loosed her hair from its ponytail.

He said that he had something to tell her, and that he wanted her to know this in advance so there would be no surprises. He said that Susan was coming to take the waters at the clinic.

Íso heard what he said, but at first she didn't understand, and then when she realized who Susan was, a hole opened up before her and she turned away. And turned back to him and said, Did you invite her?

No. She insisted. It was her choice. You have to understand. She thinks the waters might help her.

She was quiet. Then she asked, Does she know about me?

I don't want her to know about you.

You're hiding me?

No. Never. To talk about you would spoil things. She has her life, I have mine.

She said that she was confused. I don't truly know you, she said. I want to believe that you're the same man away from me as you are with me. Is that so wrong?

I'm the same, he said.

And Susan left you?

We left each other.

How long were you married?

Four years.

You must have been happy.

We were at first. She wanted to have a baby, but we couldn't. Her periods were irregular, although that's not always a problem. And so we were both tested, but there was nothing conclusive. And this made her more anxious.

And you? Were you anxious?

She called me indifferent. I called her controlling. And then we fell into our different lives. And it was easy, because she had her career and I had my work and so we became separate.

And now she is coming to you again. And she'll want to be with you. What would be the point in coming otherwise?

Many women come to the clinic and then go home without having a man.

She was quiet.

Talk to me, he said.

I don't want to be your thing.

You aren't. No. No.

It can happen. You are here and free and you find me available and you think I'm easy and besotted and so you make me your thing.

He smiled. Besotted, he said.

Is that right?

Yes, it's right. Are you besotted?

I could be. But not yet.

Let me know when you are.

She was quiet. Despite his consoling words, she was still afraid.

Riding up out of San Lucas, she was aware of Eric's body and that she was behind him and that her arms were wrapped around his waist. She felt sadness, and the sadness moved through her and she saw that it was dangerous to feel this way and so she let it go. She didn't will it away, she replaced it with acceptance. She placed her head against Eric's back and held him tight. He leaned back against her. She had always liked to wear his helmet, not only because of its physical protection but also because it provided her with some anonymity. She would appear to passersby as a figure on the back of the doctor's motorcycle—a figure that might be this person or that person, not recognizable in any clear way. She liked that her face was hidden, she liked the secrecy. But on this evening, at dusk, passing the fires beside the road, and the joggers, and the families out for an evening walk, she wished that she would be recognized, and that people would stop and say, There is Íso Perdido, riding with the doctor. As they reached the village limits, she called out to him that she didn't want to go home yet. She wanted to go to his room.

He took the back roads that wound through the upper section of the pueblo. It was dark now and all the houses were lit, and inside Íso could see a child sitting before a television, or a woman holding a baby, or a girl standing before a cooker.

He turned into the lane and they passed the restaurant of his hotel. There was a large group of people sitting near the window. She saw their gestures and their faces and she thought they were very happy.

When they arrived at his bungalow, he turned off his motorcycle and asked, Are you sure?

Yes, she said. I'm sure.


SHE sometimes wondered if their lovemaking was different for him than it was for her, and she imagined that this was true, for he was older, and he'd had his wife, and he must have had other women. This was her way of figuring out who he was and where he came from. There were moments when she saw with great clarity that Eric Mann was more alone than she was. She was surrounded by her mother, her uncles and aunts, her friends, the people in her village. He stood off to the side, tall and imposing and confident in his solitude. Others at the clinic knew of their friendship, even though she and Doctor Mann rarely spoke together at work. When they did speak, it was about a patient or some small issue that was work-related. The trip up to Tecojate with the other doctors was unusual in that Íso had been invited by Doctor Mann, and she was simply a keeper, and so an outsider, and of course it would have been obvious to Betje and Hanna and Hans that she was there because of Doctor Mann. She had reconciled all this. She did not care what people thought.

Early that week, however, the director, Elena, called her into her office and told her that the rules of the clinic were clear: the staff members weren't allowed to fraternize with the doctors. You've been spending time with Doctor Mann, Elena said.

Íso was quiet.

Is this not true? Elena asked.

We're friends, Íso said. That is true.

He's married, Elena said. Are you aware?

Yes, Íso said.

And his wife is coming here.

Yes.

What you're experiencing is not new, Elena said. This happens. A girl is attracted to a doctor who is charming, and who is from elsewhere, and who has money, and who pays attention. It's a fine thing to feel special. But then it happens that the doctor goes away and the girl is alone, and she falls into despair and her labour suffers, and I am left with a worker who has lost focus.

I'm not in despair, Íso said. She was sitting upright in her chair and listening carefully, but inside she thought that the director was wrong, and that she might even be jealous. She said again that she and the doctor were just friends.

Elena studied her for a long time, and then she said that Íso was a good keeper. One of the best. The women appreciate you, she said. You're focused.

Thank you, Íso said. She bowed her head.

Later that day, she saw him in the garden, talking to one of the patients. As she passed by he lifted a hand as if to touch her hip or to stop her, but his hand touched the patient instead. Even so, she was aware that he had noticed her.

What was more disconcerting than the viewpoint of Elena and the other workers at the clinic was the opinion of her relatives, especially her uncle Santiago, her father's eldest brother. Santiago was a woodcarver and a carpenter, one of the best in the village. He'd been involved in the construction of the clinic, and he'd carved the images of Ixchel above the lintels of the entrances to the birthing chambers. The carvings were all different. In one, Ixchel was carrying a sword and a shield. In another, she had snakes in her hair and she had jaguar claws and eyes. She was a weaver and a spider, and she was ancient.

Santiago was an artist, first and foremost. He was also temperamental and impetuous. He was protective of his niece. His carpintería sat high on the hill beside the road that led down into the village. A large window with a shuttered awning gave onto the hillside below, and on clear days the awning was lifted and there was a view of the lake and of two of the volcanoes. As a young girl Íso had loved to visit her uncle's shop. She played amongst the wood shavings, building nests into which she laid little blocks of ceiba, which were her babies. She wrote notes to her tío in the dust that had fallen onto his worktable, and he wrote her back. As she grew older, she visited less and less, but sometimes, late in the afternoon, walking home from the clinic, she went through the market and up the hill to the carpintería, where she found him and he brushed off a stool with a rag and asked her to sit.

The week that Elena spoke to her, her uncle asked her to come by his workshop. He had something for her. And so, on a Thursday, she made her way to the carpintería and found him planing a piece of wood by hand. He looked up and invited her to sit. He came to her and kissed her cheek. She smelled sawdust.

Santiago was a soft man. His face, his hands, the way he stepped along the road, his movements in his shop—all indicated a lightness of being. Even his voice was soft. He stood before Íso and removed from his front pocket a small object, to which was attached a leather thong. He held it up for Íso to see. It was a carving, from ceiba, of a white nun orchid with three petals. He said, For you, Íso, and he walked behind her and tied the thong around her neck.

When he was done and had come back to face her, she touched the carving and thanked him.

It pleases me, he said. Then he said that it was for her to remember who she was. He said that sometimes we forget. That sometimes we come face to face with an object that appears to be quite beautiful, and we are spellbound. And then we find out that the object is not so beautiful. Or it gets lost. Or it changes shape. I myself spent five years as a young man in America, he said. I understand what it is to be under a spell, and I understand disappointment.

Íso smiled. She loved her uncle. She said that she was no longer a young girl. She had her own head. And here she tapped her head with a finger. And smiled again.

This man, this doctor, her uncle said. He shook his head.

We're friends, Tío.

One day you're friends, and the next day he has hypnotized you.

I'm not hypnotized.

Not yet. But perhaps at some moment. Her uncle, as he spoke these words, had been moving lightly about his shop. To the hand planer, back to his view of the lake, returning to Íso. He stepped like a dancer, his hands raised, his wrists bent, always on the balls of his feet. His voice sounded happy. But he wasn't happy, she knew this. He was worried. It was known throughout the village that you did not upset Santiago Perdido. There were stories of his anger, and his formidable nature. There were stories about his life during the civil war, and these accounts had become legend. There were those who believed the stories, and those who didn't. Some said that Santiago was too much of an angel to be a hero. Others said that Santiago's apparent softness and his angelic looks were what made him dangerous. The recipient of Santiago's anger was always surprised.

Íso did not want to upset her uncle. She told him that Doctor Mann was only a friend. She said that Doctor Mann had a wife, and the wife was coming to visit. She shrugged. You see?

His eyes crinkled. He touched her face. He called her special. He said that he loved her. She said that she loved him as well. Very much. And she hugged him goodbye.

# 3.

AND SO THE DOCTOR'S WIFE CAME, AND ÍSO DID WHAT FOR most others would have been impossible: she cared for Susan Mann, she became her intimate other. And then Susan left the way she had come, by a car that carried her along the winding road that circled the lake, and down towards the coast and on to the city, where she would fly home. The doctor must have travelled with her, for he was absent for two days, and then he must have returned, for she saw him in the corridors of the clinic, and in the courtyard, but she did not talk to him, nor did she look at him when he passed her by.

He came to her Sunday around noon, when the churches in the village were completing their services. She was out back washing clothes and twisting the water from them and hanging them in the sunshine. Her mother called her and said that it was Doctor Mann.

She rose and walked into the dim light of the tienda and saw him standing in the entrance. She couldn't see his face, because of the sunlight behind him, but she noticed that he had a bag in his hand, and he was offering it to her. She was dressed in old clothes, and she was embarrassed to be seen like this, and she felt the beating of the blood vessel behind her right eye. He said that he'd bought a pair of boots for her, and a pair for himself. He lifted his left foot and held it up several inches above the wooden floor, and she saw the fresh yellow leather of his boots.

She looked at the bag in his hands. I can't take a gift, she said.

Why not? They won't fit me.

Maybe they'll fit your wife, she said.

She's gone, he said.

She did not speak.

Okay, tell you what. I'll keep them, and then you can come over tonight and try them on. How about that?

She shook her head. She said that she couldn't. She was busy.

Okay, how about tomorrow evening?

I'm busy then as well. She shrugged and said that she had clothes to wash. They were soaking in the tub.

She turned to leave.

He said that he had missed her. But now he was here, and he was free.

You're free, she said, but I'm not. And she went back to washing clothes. Her heart was heavy, and when she heard his motorcycle start and move up the street, she began to cry. And she thought that crying would not help, so she wiped her tears and she finished the washing. Then she swept the floor of the tienda, and she sat and cut a mango and slowly ate it, and when she was done she sucked on the pit. She went to the back and washed her face and hands and dried herself on a small towel.

That week she went to work and she returned and sat at the counter of the tienda and she went to bed and slept beside her mother, and she rose in the morning and walked through the narrow lanes to the clinic. And during those times when she was not working, and when she had time to think, she put aside her feelings and created a ledger in her head and one side was labelled True and the other was labelled False. And always, when she made her lists, she discovered that the side labelled False was full of jealousy and selfishness and fear, and so she concentrated on the True column. And on that side she wrote down all that he owned, and in doing so she moved through his life and saw herself opening the drawers where his clothing lay, and she picked up one of his shirts, and she unbuttoned it and spread it on the bed. And his socks, and his pants, and his underwear. All those articles that covered him and kept him guarded from the outside world. Las cosas del mundo. For it was things that made the world real. His world. His things. His tan boots, his motorcycle, his shaving cream and razor that lay by the mirror in his bathroom, his jeans, his wallet, his watch that he carefully removed before lying down beside her and put on again when he was finished lying with her, his eleven shirts hanging in the small closet, his running shoes, his Nike shorts, his socks balled into pairs, his deodorant, his soap in the shower, his shampoo, his belt with its bronze buckle, his driver's licence, the photograph of his mother, his nail clipper, his comb, his leather jacket and the things in the pockets of his jacket such as an American quarter and his wedding ring. When she had found the ring one day by chance, for he had asked her to look for his motorcycle keys, she held it up to the light and then laid it on his dresser top. The next time she was in the room, the ring was gone. One more thing. And on the True side she also wrote the following: He lies down with me. He eats meals with me. He talks to me. He tells me what is important. He looks at me. He calls me beautiful.

As it turned out, he visited her on Saturday evening. She was sitting with her mother in the tienda when he walked in. He spoke directly to her mother. Señora Perdido, he said, I'm riding to San Lucas tomorrow and I'd like your daughter to join me. Is that possible?

Señora Perdido had been aware of Doctor Mann's absence over the last while, and she had been aware of Íso's brooding, and so now she said that it was Íso's choice. Eric turned to Íso and asked the question. Would you come with me?

Íso nodded and said that she would be available.

In the morning there was a mist on the road, and coming down onto a flat stretch that passed through a coffee finca, she smelled the sour husk of the beans, and there was a fire at the side of the road, and two men squatted before the fire, and the light of the sun filtered through the trees and fell onto their faces, and the air was cool and then warm and then cool again. She put her arms around Eric's waist and laid her head against his back.

They sat on a verandah that overlooked the lake on which

the fishermen threw their nets. The early sun caught the drops of water as the nets fell through the air. They drank coffee and ate eggs with toast and jam and they talked about the fishermen and he talked about his research.

As she listened to him, Íso thought that Eric might be avoiding what was most important. And so, when he paused and asked if she was okay, she began to speak. She said, I always thought that when you left here, when you went back home, I would never see you again. It would be finished. Sometimes, at night, I would wake up and worry, but then I would decide that it was not good to worry—what would that help?—and I would decide that I would go through my days not thinking about the next day. I decided to love you. And then your wife came and it was revealed to me that you were not as strong as I had thought. She made you a different person. Weaker. And this made me sad. It is strange to see how different a lover can be when he is faced with an important decision, and when there is fear on his face, and when he uses words to excuse his actions. Words mean nothing. They are like the husks of the coffee bean. They cover what is essential, which is the bean itself, and when the husks are discarded, they lie on the road and rot and disappear. Actions are what lie inside, like the bean. I kept waiting for you to act, to be strong, to tell your wife that you had a lover named Íso Perdido, and that Íso was beautiful and that you wanted to be with Íso and that Íso was the most important thing in your life.

She stopped.

He said her name and reached for her hands.

She allowed this. She said that she didn't care, yes or no, if he had slept with Susan. That was past. She had her own hopes. Her own wishes. Her own desires.

Do you know why your wife loved me? Because I was nothing. It's very easy to love someone who brings you your food, who rubs your body, who never disagrees, who showers you, who says all the time yes, yes, yes. That is why she loved me. I was there and I was not there. Mostly I was not there. Invisible.

He was quiet.

You have nothing to say.

I'm surprised, he said. At your passion.

You don't know half of it, she said. And here she touched her chest. That's all, she said. I am finished.

They looked out over the water. The waiter poured more coffee. They were quiet.

Then she said, You will go home.

Yes, he said, but I prefer it here. At home I live in a safe zone surrounded by walls topped with razor wire, and there are armed guards at the gates. It's supposed to protect us, but there is always the feeling of danger. Everyone's afraid, especially those who have something to lose. The poor outnumber the wealthy and it would take only a small revolution for the poor to gain power. The only thing that stops them is the belief that they too might become rich.

Why go back?

It's home. You don't choose where you're born.

But you can choose to leave.

Yes. People do.

She found her phone and took a picture of him. And when the waiter came to remove the plates, she asked him to take a photograph of them. She gave the phone to the waiter and she rose and went over to him and she squatted beside him, and the waiter took a photograph of the two of them, with the lake in the background and the fishermen in their boats and the mist rising off the water.

She took the phone back from the waiter and thanked him and she went back to her seat. She looked at the photograph and then handed him the phone and he looked at it and she said that she would send it to him. To remember this time.

He handed the phone back to her and said that he didn't need a photograph to remember this time.

A path opened before her, but the path was narrow and hard to follow, and she thought that if she said anything more, she might lose sight of him on the path, and so she said nothing.

Leaving San Lucas, he took a different route and they rode up around the lake towards the highway that would take them to either Antigua or Panajachel. The road was rough and full of potholes, and she had to hold tightly to his waist, and when she did so he pushed his body back towards her so that they were as one. They stopped by the roadside, high above the lake, and they sat on a guardrail with their feet on the cliffside, where there grew chicozapote and puna and ciprés, and far below was the lake, which was calm. In the distance a boat made its way towards her village.

They didn't speak. She took his hand and held it and she thought of all the lovers who had sat in this exact spot and looked down at the lake, which had existed for thousands of years. And she thought that the lake and the volcanoes around the lake, which were all beautiful, and inspired one to speak of their beauty, were indifferent to beauty, and they were indifferent to her own existence and her own desires. She was the only one who knew and cared about her own existence, and her own wishes, and her own desires.

She wanted to explain this to Eric, but she didn't have the words, or perhaps she was afraid that he wouldn't understand. She said, I'm very happy to be me and not that tree, or that rock, or even this large lake. And with this statement she flung her arm out towards the lake.

You don't know *the* half of it, he said. What you said before. You forgot the *the*.

Thank you, Mr. Teacher, she said. She touched his forehead and said that she wanted to know what was in there.

He said that she was everything in his head.

These words, said so casually, stunned her.

THEY stole as much time as possible for each other. One Saturday they rode down to Monterico and sat in a restaurant where they ate crab and shrimp, and in the evening, when the mosquitoes were too much, they found their small room and made love as the fan blew hot air over their sweating bodies. After, he fell asleep immediately, but she was restless and hot and the only clear thought she could muster was that she was incapable of thinking clearly. She got up and peed, and as she sat on the toilet she realized that she had been peeing a lot in the last while. She lit a candle and placed it on the table beside the bed and in that flickering light she studied him. He always slept as if completely innocent. It seemed so wasteful, to be sleeping when they had so little time together. She wanted to rouse him and hold him and she wanted to ask him if he loved her. She had asked him that just before he slept, and he had kissed her forehead and called her silly. Of course I love you, he said. It was dark, and she could not see his eyes, and she realized that lately he had confessed his love only in the darkness, and so she had been unable to look into his eyes and verify his words. For the eyes cannot lie. They shift sideways and close, or they blink, or the gaze is averted, and she realized that it might have been her fear all along that he was being untruthful, because she asked the question only when they were in darkness.

And now, she lit the candle, and she studied his body and his head and his hair and shoulders. The sheet lay across his lower body and she saw the hair at his stomach, which she loved to touch, and she saw his chest and one long arm thrown up above his head. Who are you? she whispered. She was ashamed to doubt him. It was not in her nature. Nor was it in her nature to light a candle in the darkness, or to rummage through his pockets, or to steal his hair from his comb. Sometimes she saw herself as a madwoman, though she was only twenty-two.

Their bungalow was situated near the beach and she heard the waves come in and recede and then rush in again onto the sand. She heard the voices of a man and a woman as they passed by the open window. The man was saying something about his shoes. Íso was sitting cross-legged on the bed and she heard the voices and she thought that if her father had not died when she was just a child, she would have known the quality of a man's voice, other than Eric's, and she might have known how a man's inner thoughts worked. Or if a man had inner thoughts. Tonight, Eric had felt far away, as if he had already left. As if his thinking was already in another country, with those things that awaited him.

She fell asleep.

And woke to the sound of the couple fighting about the shoes. At first she believed it was a dream, and then she was awake, and the man was shouting that they were not his shoes, he'd never seen them before, and if they weren't his, where had they come from? The woman said that he was drunk and that he had probably bought the shoes in Pastores and forgotten that fact. The man said that he'd never been to Pastores in his life. He said that the shoes were too big on him, and why would he buy shoes that were two sizes too big? The woman said that he was fond of big things, and that was why he had bought shoes that were too big. And then the woman's voice went soft and she whispered something that Íso could not hear. But the man would have nothing of it. He shouted, Look here, look here. This is not my shoe. And if it isn't my shoe, whose is it? Are these Hugo's? The one with big feet? His voice was sad and high and he began to cry. The woman shushed him some more and said that he should leave the shoes in the sand if they weren't his. It's hot, she said. Come, come to bed. Forget the shoes.

Íso didn't hear the couple leave, but she thought they had moved on because now all she heard was the surf, which sounded like a wind that was starting up and then subsiding and then starting up again.

THEY ate breakfast at a comedor on the beach—scrambled eggs and tortillas and fresh pineapple and refried beans. He had slept well. And you? he asked. She said that she had been very hot and the air had been stuffy and there had been people walking loudly past their window. And a couple arguing about shoes. She told him what had transpired. She wanted it to sound interesting, or even a little bit funny, but he found it neither interesting nor funny, and when she had finished the story he asked if the shoes were in the sand by their bungalow. Did he leave them there? he asked.

I never looked, she said.

That is what would finish the story, he said. If they were lying in the sand.

I don't think so, she said. Why does the story have to be finished?

Because if it isn't finished, it isn't a story.

It might be finished in a different way, she said. The man might have thrown the shoes into the water.

Or the woman might have.

This thought was surprising to her, but it didn't seem surprising to him. She looked at his eyes, but he was busy eating. They saw the world in different ways. For him, life was like a story that had answers, or a conclusion that made sense. For her, the story was sinuous and unclear, and if there was happiness to be had, it might arrive unannounced, or it might land in the arms of another person.

Later, they found themselves on the beach, and he touched her, and talked to her, and throughout all his close attention she felt as if she were floating above the scene, looking down on the man and the girl on the beach. She was very quiet and he asked if she was okay and she said that she was tired. She hadn't slept well. At noon they packed and climbed on the motorcycle and rode the five hours back towards the village. Ascending the hills, she was relieved to be leaving the humidity and heat behind her. She'd been lonely in Monterico. Perhaps it was because of the little flies that attacked during the hottest part of the day. Or the mosquitoes. Or the tourists. On the back of the motorcycle, holding him, she still felt very much alone.

SHE sometimes chided him for driving too fast. Behind him on the motorcycle, she would grip his waist and shout at him to slow down, and he always did. When he was with her. She knew that when he was alone, riding the back roads or taking the coastal route to the city, he rode even faster, and often without a helmet. He loved the wind and the danger. He said that it made him feel alive.

Tuesday of that week, after a long ride alone into the hills, he was returning at dusk, his hair blowing free, and just as he came up out of San Lucas, before the long climb, he hit a child. The child was chasing a dog that had run out onto the road and Eric hit the dog first and his motorcycle went out from under him and he flew off and his body hit the child, killing the child instantly. Eric was not wearing a helmet, and though the body of the child broke his fall, he still hit the road heavily, first his shoulder, which broke, and then his head, which gave off the sound of a soft thud, a simple sound, but important. Momentum carried him into the concrete culvert beside the road.

The boy who had been killed came from a family whose father picked coffee at a nearby finca and went into the hills on the weekends to gather wood to sell as fuel in San Lucas. The boy was five years old, the youngest of ten children. His name was Juan. The father was eating supper in his small house when word came that Juan had been hit by a motorcycle and was lying in the road. The driver of the motorcycle was also in the road. They were both dead.

When the father arrived at the scene, he picked up his son and cradled him, and kissed his forehead and his face and he called out for him to breathe. But the boy was limp and lifeless. The father carried him to the side of the road and placed him in the dirt beneath a shrub. Someone brought a blanket and laid it over the boy. A voice called out that the driver of the motorcycle was alive. By now, a crowd had gathered. The father of the dead boy found the motorcycle driver sitting up at the edge of the road, calling out, Soy médico, soy médico. He's a doctor, someone shouted. The father took the doctor's hair in his hands and pulled him to his feet. He cursed at him. He called for a rope. A few minutes later a young man appeared with a rope and handed it to the father. The father looped the rope around Doctor Mann's neck and tied it tight. He dragged him towards a nearby eucalyptus tree that had a branch that was solid and perfectly parallel to the ground. By now others in the crowd were chanting and calling out. Some were kicking at Doctor Mann's body, at his arms, and when they found the mark, especially his broken shoulder, he whimpered. His pants were pulled down. There was laughter. The doctor said, Soy americano, and then he said, Estados Unidos. For a moment the crowd paused, but it made little difference that this man was an American. He had recklessly killed a child of theirs, and so they converged on him once again.

They would have lynched him if the pastor of the evangelical church in San Pedro, Carlos Iclash, who was also the owner of the small coffee finca where the dead boy's father worked, hadn't been passing by on a return trip from the city. The road was blocked as Señor Iclash approached the scene. Carlos stopped his pickup and rolled down his window and asked a young girl what was happening. Linchamiento, the girl said. Un americano. Carlos carried a pistol. Because he believed it was necessary. He took the pistol from his bag and got out of the pickup and approached the rabble. The people were very excited, like children at a circus. He pushed his way into the crowd. He fired a shot in the air. The crowd halted and then set to again. He pushed through to the inner circle and walked over to the father of the dead boy. The man was pulling at the rope, which he'd strung over the branch of the eucalyptus. He was hoisting the American by the neck, and the American's legs were kicking at the air. Carlos held the pistol to the father's head and told him to release the man.

He killed my son, the father said.

Release him, Carlos said. This isn't for you to decide. There will be proper justice.

The father looked Carlos in the eyes and said that he would release the man, but only because Carlos Iclash had promised justice. And he lowered the body of the doctor. Carlos called out to the crowd to go home. The mob, grumpy and disappointed, mumbled and then slowly dispersed. Carlos bent to inspect the doctor. The doctor was unconscious. He removed the noose. He pulled up the doctor's pants. He asked for help to carry the body to his pickup. No one offered him help. He stooped and picked up the doctor. It was difficult, and he dropped him twice before he managed to hoist him over his shoulder. He walked back to the pickup and laid him in the bed of the truck. Carlos climbed back into his pickup and drove to the clinic at Ixchel, where he knew there were qualified doctors.

Íso heard the following morning that Doctor Mann had been driven to the city, and that he was in surgery at one of the private clinics there. Her manager told her the details of the accident, and of the attack. She worked that day, but her heart was elsewhere. At noon she sat in the garden and she put her face in her hands, making certain that no one saw her. She knew nothing about Eric's condition.

The following morning when she arrived at work, she asked after the doctor. Her relationship with him was seen as friendly. It was not known how deeply she cared for him. And he for her. And so she had to pretend that she was simply concerned because he was popular, and they were friends. The news was that he had suffered a broken clavicle and he had some swelling on the brain. He would be okay. She was amazed at her relief. At the end of the day she found Illya, and Illya, who had heard about the accident, hugged her, and it was then that Íso cried and cried as Illya spoke softly into her ear.

What will happen? Íso asked.

He will live, Illya said. Don't worry.

Poor Eric, she said.

The following morning she arrived early at work and asked again after the doctor. She was told that the doctor's wife had been contacted, and that she might arrive soon. Or she would come later. In any case, it was clear that the doctor's wife would be making an appearance. When she told Illya, Illya said that she should go to see him as soon as possible. The next day was Friday, and even though there was work, she should go. Illya said she would tell the director that Íso was not well. She hugged Íso again, and said, You must.

And so on Friday morning, she went with her mother to visit Doctor Mann. They rode the boat across the lake in the early morning and took a bus up to Sololá and transferred to another bus that would take them into the city. It took a long time to reach the main highway, and after many stops they turned onto the Panamericana. She held her mother's hand and they looked out at the fields and as they ascended the highlands a mist enveloped them and it began to rain and the world disappeared.

The doctor was in a private hospital that resembled an expensive hotel. It was silent and spotless and there was no poverty to be

seen on the faces of those who whispered through the halls. The
floors were of hardwood and ceramic, and the chairs in the waiting
room were of leather. Her mother sat in one of these chairs while
she made inquiries at the front desk. Íso would be allowed to see
the doctor for ten minutes.

A nurse guided Íso to the elevator and then took her to the
third floor. The nurse was young and she had a strong jaw and
she didn't say much to Íso except to state that Doctor Mann was
known here. He is very fortunate, she said.

Will he live? Íso asked.

The nurse looked at her as if she were crazy. Of course, she
said. Then she said that Doctor Mann did not like to be touched.
It upset him. Íso nodded. She could not imagine Eric not wanting
to be touched.

He was sitting up in bed. The nurse went in first and told him
that he had a visitor and announced her as Íso. His face, when he
saw her, registered no surprise or curiosity, and it was as if she
were a stranger. She went to him and told him again that she was
Íso. He repeated her name several times, as if it were a game. The
nurse remained in the room, but this did not stop Íso from standing near his bed and saying his name. His neck was bruised and
she put her hand near his throat and asked if it hurt. He shook his
head. She was crying. And then she said that all was good, wasn't
it? You're alive, she said.

Look at you, she said. Your hair.

It had been cut. He looked like a young boy. Smaller and more
vulnerable. His arm was in a sling.

She had many questions, but she didn't ask them, because the nurse was present and because he couldn't move past her name, which he said again and again, as if it were something new that he had just learned.

And she said his name, Eric, over and over. And their ten minutes was wasted speaking each other's name, and saying nothing of importance. And not touching. When the nurse said that Íso's time was up, that the patient needed to rest, Doctor Mann seemed confused. His eyes looked tired. She wanted to ask the surgeon in charge if Doctor Mann would be okay—she didn't trust the nurse—but she couldn't locate anyone who might give her a clear answer, and so she and her mother left the hospital and returned to the village.

When she went back alone to the hospital the following weekend, his wife was there, and when she saw the wife she knew that everything was over. The doctor's wife was feeding him puréed apples from a small bowl, lifting a spoon to his mouth, whispering something that Íso could not understand. He looked even more like a child. He ate slowly. When the doctor's wife saw Íso, she stood and went to her and hugged her, holding her tightly, and then she stepped back and said, I'm taking him home.

Íso didn't say anything.

She sat beside the doctor's wife and held her hand while the doctor held his wife's hand, and so in some distant way there was a connection. The doctor's wife told her husband that Íso, her keeper, had come for a visit.

Hello, Íso, Eric said.

Hello, Eric.

He looked at her, and then he looked at his wife, who reached out to wipe saliva from his bottom lip.

Íso freed her hand, but the doctor's wife didn't seem to notice.

He'll have to have rehabilitation, she said. He has trouble walking. And he's suffered trauma to the brain. He can't remember anything about the accident. At first he didn't even know my name. What a terrible story, she said. What a godforsaken place. They want to press charges or something horrible. But we have a lawyer and the lawyer says that the sooner he goes home, the better chance we have of no charges being laid. And so we'll go home. She leaned towards the doctor and whispered, Isn't that right, Eric?

Íso watched all this with horror.

When will you take him? Íso asked.

As soon as possible. He'll be ready to fly next week.

Is that what he wants? Íso asked. It was a bold question, but she needed to ask it.

What he wants is impossible to say. He can't make decisions right now. He needs proper care.

Íso had no words left. She rose, and then she walked around behind the doctor's wife and approached the bed and she leaned over Doctor Mann and she looked into his eyes. Goodbye, Eric, she said. And she kissed him on the mouth. His face was blank.

Íso stepped back. She walked past Susan, who was standing now, her head tilted, her eyes surprised. Íso walked past her and out of the room. She left the hospital and stepped into the street and walked for a long time until she came to a small park, where she found a bench. She sat down. She folded her hands in her lap. The sun fell onto her head. It was very warm. She removed her jacket and laid it across her lap. She folded her hands again. And she wept.

# 4.

FOR A TIME AFTER HIS DEPARTURE SHE SURVIVED ON MEMORIES. The trips to the pueblos, the sound of his motorcycle approaching, a glimpse of him walking along the paths at the clinic. She heard his motorcycle everywhere, but especially in the evenings as she sat inside the tienda and the traffic moved up the street towards the market. Always, when she heard the sound of his motorcycle, she would look up and wait for him to walk through the door, but of course he was gone.

She had his contact information, which he'd given to her before the accident, and one day she sat down and typed up a message and sent it. She kept everything simple. She talked about the clinic, and the staff, and she said that he was missed. She said that she was still studying on Saturdays, and that she was reading Shakespeare. She didn't understand it very well. She said that her work was regular, and the women were all the same. They were still *hungry*. He had used that word to describe the women at the clinic, and she imagined that the word might spark something in him. She said that she hoped he was recovering. Tell me about yourself, she said. And say hello to your wife.

She added the last part because she was certain that the doctor's wife would be screening his mail. She waited for a response, but nothing came.

Three months passed. She felt wild and hollow. And then she did something she had not thought possible: she spent some time with Illya's cousin Roberto, who was from Argentina and was living in Panajachel during his school break. Íso had first met him at Illya's wedding. There were two weddings, one in Buenos Aires, and a second, smaller version in Panajachel. Íso was invited to the second wedding, which was a dinner and dance. She bought a dress that was loose and teal blue and quite modest—the hemline fell to her knees—and she wore a necklace of her mother's, and blue pumps. The day was windy and she had to hold her hair in place as she rode the boat across the lake.

At the reception she danced with Illya, and she danced with two or three boys whose bodies felt immature. Their minds were empty. It was not their fault. She had been spoiled.

Roberto was slightly older, in university studying law, and he found her near the end of the evening and they talked in a back corner at a small table. He talked about himself mostly, and she listened to him and she did not listen. He was very good looking, with a convincing jaw and beautiful eyes and delicate hands. He went out to smoke, and she walked out with him and they stood in the shadows as he smoked and talked about the differences between their countries. He said that the poverty was more evident here. The politics are backwards, he said. Though we have our own despots as well. They were speaking Spanish, of course. He showed her a tattoo on his shoulder. Unbuttoned his shirt and pulled down the shirt and told her that this was his mother's name. Alejandra. He said that it had been difficult to find space on his shoulder for the number of letters in his mother's name, but it was okay. What do you think? he asked.

It's good, she said.

And you? he asked. Do you have a tattoo?

She laughed and shook her head.

Illya does, he said.

Of course.

He put out his cigarette and touched her face. You're unhappy, he said.

No. I'm happy, she said.

I don't think so.

She shrugged.

What would make you happy? he asked.

She said the answer to that was impossible.

He bent to kiss her and she let him. She was curious, that was all. He tasted of cigarettes and she smelled a perfume on him. He did not put his tongue inside her mouth, though she wouldn't have minded. She held the back of his head and was aware that he was shorter than Eric.

He pulled away and said, Happier now?

I'm happy, she said.

They went back inside and they danced, and then Illya appeared and she danced with them as well, and then Illya and Roberto danced and Íso sat down and watched them.

It is over, she thought.

She saw Roberto again, and was free with him, and slept with him two times, even though she was constantly thinking about Eric. She had not yet told anyone about the baby. One evening, a few weeks earlier, she had stopped at a farmacia where she did not know the owners and they did not know her, and she had purchased a pregnancy test. She went home and locked herself in the bathroom and took out the tester and peed. It verified what she already knew. She sat for a long time in the bathroom and tried to think logically about what she must do, but then she thought of Eric and she felt sad for what might have been. She pushed these thoughts away, because what good could come of them, and what purpose might they serve other than to make her wilder in her sadness? She wrapped the tester in a piece of tissue and she put it in her pocket. She would discard it later, away from home.

She took to wearing looser clothing, but then she was with Roberto and she could not hide it from him. He said that he had always wanted to make love to a pregnant woman. He was like an overgrown adolescent. He had no sense of consequence. After a few more occasions she said that a relationship wasn't possible.

Illya met her one day after work and said that Roberto had told her, and how was it that Roberto knew before she did? God,

Íso, she said. Look at you. And she touched Íso's belly. When? she asked.

In sixteen weeks.

It is Doctor Mann's?

Illya. She said this sharply, in annoyance or shame, or both.

Have you told him?

Why? He's gone.

Has he written?

Nothing.

Because of his wife. Or perhaps he's still sick.

Íso said that she didn't want to think about it.

Will you have the baby at the clinic?

Yes, but in a regular room. I couldn't stand knowing there were people behind the glass watching.


Íso began to make plans. She took the bus to the city one Saturday and she picked up an application for permit papers for herself. And then she went to the US embassy and inquired about registration for a child who was born outside the country.

The woman she spoke with wore very large and round glasses on a very narrow face that looked like a machete. The woman asked if she was a United States citizen.

No, Íso said, but the father is.

The woman said that then the father would have to apply for the passport and for the citizenship papers after the child was born.

I cannot?

No, ma'am. You cannot. She appeared to be mocking Íso's speech. Then she said that Íso might want to let the father know.

Íso was startled and she looked down. I will, she said.

But she didn't. She imagined that the doctor's wife was reading his mail, and she didn't want the doctor's wife to know anything. She put aside her permit application. She tried to forget about him.

And there came a time when she could no longer hide what was real, and so she told her mother, who said that she already knew. She had been waiting for Íso to tell her. Her mother saw the world as a place you walked through in your own way, and as long as you cared for others and yourself, no matter what difficulties you encountered, you took what was given to you, and you accepted it. She asked if Doctor Mann knew about the baby.

He doesn't, Íso said.

Her mother asked if she would tell him.

If he wants to know, I'll tell him.

How will you know what he wants?

He'll let me know.


SEÑORA Perdido had never spoken to Íso of her life between the ages of eighteen and twenty-one, when she walked away from her home on the shores of the lake. But one evening, she closed the tienda early, and she sat across from Íso at the table in their small kitchen, and she said that she had a story to tell her. It was an important story for Íso to hear, because it would reveal to her something about the ways of the world, and it would give her information with which she might make her own decisions. Señora Perdido said that some of it Íso had heard before, but that now she would tell Íso everything, even if what she said might sound too intimate or even wrong and unfortunate.

At that time, she said, I was a few years younger than you are now. She said that her own father had been very handsome and tall, and her mother pretty and short. They were quite a sight walking side by side. Her father had come from Catalonia, in Spain, and he had fallen in love with the people of the country, and of course he had fallen in love with his bride. The civil war had gone on for many years and her father was very political and very strong in his views and he spoke out against the taking of land and the killings and the disappearances. He didn't carry a gun, he wasn't violent, but he was known to have fervent opinions, and for this reason he wasn't liked by those in power. And her father was killed. And her mother was killed. And then her brother, Íso's uncle, left to fight with the rebels. He was gone, and so she was alone.

One day a boy came to the village and told her that her brother was dead. The army had killed him. They had taken out his eyes and cut out his tongue and then shot him and hanged him from a ceiba tree. The boy told her to leave. And so she put some clothes into her bag and she left.

I was eighteen years old, she said.

Because the army was everywhere, and she had no one to trust, she walked around the lake rather than taking the public boat. In Sololá she took a bus north, and two days later she crossed over into Mexico at Tapachula. For three weeks she travelled up through Mexico by foot and by bus and entered the United States at Laredo. She said that in those days the border was not yet sealed, and so those without papers were able to find a way across. At first she felt lost in the United States of America, but what was the point of feeling lost? Or lonely? She was safe. Her father had visited San Francisco and he had talked of its beauty, and not knowing where else to go, she asked a man how to get to San Francisco. He told her about Greyhound, and so she rode a bus called Greyhound and arrived in San Francisco. She walked the streets. She learned that there was food in the garbage bins behind the supermarkets. She slept in parks and discovered the outdoor children's pools, where she could wash herself. One afternoon, in a park, a man introduced himself. He spoke some Spanish, but not very well, and so he spoke English and she spoke Spanish, and this was how they talked. Henry was a good man in some ways, but he wasn't good in other ways. He was generous with ideas and conversation, but he was also greedy and jealous. Like all men, he offered one thing in order to take something else. And that something else was usually the soul of the woman. And so, Henry took her by the arm and said, Come. He bought her breakfast at a small café.

This was the first time she ate a waffle, which was like a pancake, but not the same. Two days later, or maybe it was longer, he found her a job washing dishes at a hotel. So now she had a little money. She was sleeping on the streets at the time, in a cardboard house under a bridge, and Henry said that was far too dangerous and he said she could move in with him. Señora Perdido said she was happy enough under the bridge. Which wasn't completely true, but she knew that she hadn't run all this way to America to end up in the arms of a man she did not love. She was also aware of her mother and father and brother and how they would see her if they were still living. She knew a girl, called Lan, who worked at the hotel and was always smoking on her breaks. Her voice was like a ringing bell. Lan had some space in her apartment, and invited her to live there. On Saturdays, when they were not working, they walked along the wharf and watched the boats and talked about which boat they would buy.

She still saw Henry and on Sundays they walked over the Golden Gate Bridge and sat on a wooden dock and Henry fished while she read. She was learning to read English and Henry had many westerns. She liked them. She wanted to ride a horse. Meet a cowboy. Henry was not a cowboy. He painted houses for a living. She washed dishes at a hotel. Life was very different, but she was still Luisa. This is what happens, she told Íso. Nothing happens. You are who you are.

One day she signed up for an English course. She met people like her. People who didn't speak English. People who were strangers. People from China and India. There was a girl from Africa who was very thin and very tall.

She wrote her assignments in a journal that she handed in to the professor, an older man named Lewis, who, when he read her writing, said that she had more to say than any of the students he had taught over the past ten years. She didn't quite understand his enthusiasm, but when she told Henry, on one of the Sunday afternoons on the wharf, all Henry said was, He wants you. She had no interest in her professor. She had no interest in Henry. Lan, with whom she was still living, thought it was great, all this romantic interest, and she asked which of the two men had more money. This was how Lan saw the world.

One night after class, she went out with several classmates and the professor joined them. He sat beside her and talked about his life. For a time he had lived in Canada, in Vancouver, where he married and had a child. And then he moved back to San Francisco and settled in and he was now alone. He said the word "alone" with great gravity and she wondered if it was true that he wanted her. It concerned her that he had a child out there somewhere, because if it was true that he couldn't take care of a child, then what did that say about the other rules in his life.

The kitchen in which Íso and her mother sat had one light that hung from the ceiling, and at this point Íso stood and found a candle and she lit the candle and turned off the overhead light. Now her mother's face was darker, and the flame flickered and threw shadows, but it felt safer. She took two glasses and poured water in both, and she handed her mother a glass and sat down and took her own glass and drank. Thank you, her mother said. She took some water, and continued to speak.

When the course was finished she said goodbye to her new friends and to Lewis. For a year she shared the apartment with Lan. She washed dishes. She bought some new clothes. She went to the library and read books for free. She was happy enough. Sometimes she went to dances at a Spanish club, but the boys there reminded her of her brother, she said, who was dead.

And then, one afternoon, on the boardwalk by the ocean, Lewis found her. She was eating fish and chips when he walked by with a woman on his arm. He stopped and said her name and she looked up and saw him and it was very strange because she was both confused and happy. The woman on his arm was his age, maybe a bit younger. This was Laura, his sister. Lewis and Laura had the same nose. He wanted her address and he gave her paper on which to write it. He asked for a phone number as well. She didn't have a phone. An address is adequate, he said. This was how he talked and she recalled that she liked the way he spoke, with words that she didn't always understand. His sister stood off to the side and watched the seagulls and crossed her feet like sophisticated and pretty women do. Then Lewis shook Luisa's hand and said goodbye.

He dropped by to find her two weeks later. He was wearing a blue sweater and an orange scarf. The scarf made him look younger. He said that he was still teaching ESL. He asked if she wanted to get a drink, or something to eat. She said that she didn't drink. Fine, he said, we'll eat then. They went to a small Italian restaurant. She had never been to an Italian restaurant—in fact, she had not been to a sit-down restaurant other than those places on the wharf where she ordered fish and chips and sat at picnic tables and chased away the gulls. He ordered spaghetti for them. And a bottle of wine. He poured himself a glass and then poured a small amount for her as well. Try it, he said. She found it dry and sour. Still, she finished it and he poured her some more. She told Íso that this was the first and the last time she became drunk, and she sometimes thought later that if she had not had wine that night, many things would have been different in her life, though she did not know if her life would have been better or worse. The wine gave her a pleasant feeling and when Lewis took her hand and asked if she would look at his apartment, she said yes. They sat on the hardwood floor in his living room and talked until midnight and drank more wine. He burned candles, she said, much like the candle that is burning here on the table. She waved a hand at the candle, as if it might be chased away, but it kept burning.

She said that Lewis kept telling her she was beautiful, and she asked him what he meant. You have dark hair, he said, and dark eyes, and I like your face, and I like your thoughts, and I like to hear your thoughts. He was very impractical. Or perhaps he was a dreamer. She thought this was funny. She didn't see herself as beautiful. She was too tall and her mouth was too wide. And then he said that he liked her, very much. She told him that she liked him too, he was a nice man.

More than nice, he said, and he tried to kiss her. She pushed him away, gently at first, but he wouldn't listen, he became stronger, and finally he was too strong and he took her by the throat and pushed her onto the floor. It was not love. And later, walking home alone, she passed by strange men—men whom she might have considered dangerous before, but who now seemed normal. She was crying, but no one spoke or said anything to her. In fact, they turned away. She told no one. Not the police, not Lan. And eventually she began to imagine that nothing bad had happened, and she wondered if she had made up the story in her own head.

There was something about living in a country where the language was not yours. You appeared to be stupid, and you weren't noticed. Or if you were noticed, it was for your body, or to clean someone's toilet, or to look after someone's child. You turned into someone to chase or to scorn or to look down on. It was necessary, wherever you lived, to have the poor so that everyone else felt better. You want to know a poor woman, she said to Íso, look at her hands. And she held up her hands for Íso to see, but the light was dim, and in the darkness her hands looked young. Íso took them and held them as her mother continued to speak.

She said that when she met Diego, he saw only her face, and he spoke to her tenderly of her beauty and he held her rough-looking hands, unaware of both her physical and her spiritual poverty. She said that she met him at a dance for those who spoke Spanish. Though there were also boys there who didn't speak Spanish. Most of the boys had come to meet a muchacha. The girls were popular, and these boys thought the girls were simple and easy, but they weren't. She noticed Diego right away. He was a good dancer. His hair was combed back and it was shining and he wore leather shoes and a beautiful soft pale shirt and his smile was devastating. And she felt safe for the first time. He worked in the valley picking asparagus, moving from farm to farm, and on Sundays he drove all the way into San Francisco to find her and this is how he wooed her. He invited her to join him. She did. They travelled the countryside, and on weekends they went to the coast and walked on the beach and put their feet into the water. For a year their life was full and rich, even though the money they had was little. He showed her a piece of land that he one day wanted to own. How much is it? she asked. Too much, he said. One Sunday they ate a picnic on a blanket on that land, in the shade of a tree, and pretended that the land was theirs. All was hopeful. That afternoon, on the drive home, the police stopped them because the tail light was broken on Diego's pickup. They were arrested and put in holding for three weeks, and during that time she did not have contact with Diego. She heard that he was sent back to Mexico, and a week later she was sent back to her own country.

She never saw Diego again. She tried to contact him in his village in southern Mexico, but there was no response. So now she put the past behind her and she concentrated on the future. She found a job cooking and washing clothes for the family of the man who would become Íso's father, a man who had lived in the village all his life, a man a little older than she was. He had never left the country, and he was a local boy who had grown up poor, but he had managed to make enough money to put a down payment on a van, and so he started his own business. That was the man she married. And he became your father, she said. He was not like the other men she had known. No lies, sweet nonsense, and then anger. No big dreams of America and a piece of land. He was gentle. He loved me. And we had you, Íso. And you, because of him, will have more than I ever had. You are smarter, and you are better inside, and you will not make the same mistakes that I made. Do you see? Then she said that her story had been too long, and that possibly it had not made any sense.

It made sense, Íso said. It made me sad. And then she asked her mother why she had waited so long to tell her this story. She said that if she had known sooner, she might have been wiser.

Señora Perdido said that wisdom was earned. It didn't come from hearing stories of other people's lives. Even now, she said, you'll make decisions that will take you down a difficult road. And she squeezed Íso's hands. Íso thought that her mother was very beautiful at that moment, and she experienced the thrill of being a confidante, one into whose soul has been poured the many secrets of the teller.

# 5.

As typically happened with keepers who were pregnant, Íso became popular with the women who came to take the waters. She was aware of being studied and admired. There was always one woman each day who asked if she might touch Íso. She allowed this. What followed were questions about how far along she was, and was the baby moving, and was it a girl or a boy. She didn't know the gender and she said that yes, the baby was moving. This happened more and more at night as she lay in bed beside her mother. The baby threw itself around in her womb. And she would take her mother's hand and place it on her belly and say, Here.

And they laughed together.

She was constantly hungry. She found herself eating at night, late, and waking with heartburn, for which she took aloe juice. And during the day, if the woman she had served left any food on her

plate, she ate that as well, in secret. She was very fond of raw veget-
ables and always had a carrot at hand. Her back began to ache. Her
ankles and knees. Her work became more trying, though the time
in the pool was a relief.

No one at the clinic except Illya truly knew who the father was,
though the other keepers certainly would have guessed, and Elena
as well. If there was any gossip, she ignored it. One time when she
happened to be working with Betje, Betje asked about the father,
and she used Eric's name, but Íso pretended that she hadn't heard
the question, and she turned away and made herself busy.

She thought often of Eric and imagined him as he was before
he left, before the accident, and she found herself doubting
everything that had happened between them. His body, her name
in his mouth, his hands, and his hair flying out behind him as he
rode his motorcycle. All was a dream. She wrote letters to him
that she did not send, long letters describing the development of
the baby, explaining that the girl (for she imagined it was a girl)
would now have fingernails, and eyelids, and a brain, and hair. She
said that the little girl would have wonderful hair. Imagine. Always,
after she finished one of these letters, she saved it and closed down
her computer, and the letters became like her thoughts, for herself
only, unspoken, not to be shared.

During one two-week block she cared for a Frenchwoman who
spoke no English and only a little Spanish, and so they communic-
ated by touch and gestures and with their eyes and with a shared
elementary vocabulary. The woman's name was Odette. She was a
slight woman, with a crooked back and dark eyes. Her husband was

at home, running the family business. He planned to come within the week. Odette was always asking to touch Íso, and she allowed this, but it was clear that Odette could not see that she was more than a womb carrying a fetus. Odette asked one time if she could put her ear to Íso's belly. She would like to listen. She touched her ear and then touched Íso. Yes? she asked.

Íso allowed this. She lifted her blouse and Odette laid her head against Íso's belly. She was quite large by now, and Odette was very small, and for a moment, looking down at her, Íso thought that Odette resembled a doll, or an infant herself. Íso said, Okay, and she lowered her top. Odette was lying on her back on the massage table. She was trembling.

Íso had learned that a woman's mouth will signal her personality. A wide mouth meant a generous woman. An undersized mouth indicated miserliness, a person who was always taking. Odette's mouth was undersized and thin.

The following morning, the director, Elena, spoke with Íso. She called her into her office and asked her to sit down. Íso had not been in Elena's office since that day when Elena laid out the rules about fraternizing with the doctors. And now, here they were, both of them aware that she had not told the truth about Doctor Mann. But it was too late now. The road had been chosen.

Elena wore a black-and-white sleeveless dress with a pearl necklace. Íso was wearing her blue smock and her sandals. She felt diminished.

Elena asked how Íso was feeling.

Íso said that she was good. Strong.

And the baby? It's strong?

Íso nodded.

You're big, Elena said. Chubby. She said that it was important to gain weight. Then she said that a request had come from a patient regarding a contract for Íso's baby.

What do you mean? Íso asked. She knew exactly what Elena meant, but she couldn't think clearly and so she asked the question.

Someone is interested in your baby.

Who? Odette?

As you know, Íso, we never release names.

I'm not interested, Íso said.

They're offering a large amount.

There is no amount large enough.

You will want to think on it, Elena said, and she waved a hand casually, as if they might have been talking about the purchase of tortillas or a handful of limes in the market.

No, Íso said, I won't want to think on it.

Elena appeared disappointed. She said, I see that you wish to have the baby here, in one of the private rooms.

Yes.

That's good. It means so much to the clients when our keepers use the premises. A sense of trust and faith. Is it a girl or a boy?

I don't know.

I never wanted to know the gender of my children. It can be like a little game, full of anticipation and curiosity.

This was the first time Íso had heard Elena speak of her children. She felt off balance.

Elena asked if Doctor Mann knew about the baby.

Íso was quiet. She saw Elena's fingers playing with the pearls at her chest. Her fingers were quite fat, like little chorizo sausages.

It was clear that he loved you, Elena said.

Íso lifted her head.

And that you loved him.

She had no words, her thoughts were confused.

Elena asked again if Doctor Mann knew about the baby.

Íso said that she hadn't heard from the doctor. He had completely disappeared.

He's still recovering, Elena said. His head. And here she waved at her own head.

You spoke with him? Íso asked.

With his wife.

Does she know? About the baby?

If she doesn't, she should. As should the doctor. Isn't that reasonable? The fact is, Íso, you went against the rules of the clinic. And now you seem to think that the baby is yours alone. That you single-handedly created it. You have too much pride.

I don't think so.

Elena said that it would be best to write Doctor Mann and tell him about his child. He had a right to know.

Íso found it hard to breathe. She placed her hands on her stomach, and bowed her head. I'll write and tell him, she said.

Good, Elena said. She looked at her watch, which was oversized and made of silver. She lowered her arm. She waited.

Íso realized that the conversation was over. She stood and excused herself. In the hallway she walked slowly, holding her belly.

That day, in the pool, she wanted to drown Odette. Push her

miniature mouth under the water and hold it until all the French bubbles had disappeared. Instead, she whispered soft words of hope and relaxation. Odette's eyes were closed. She breathed deeply. In the bath, she asked again to touch Íso.

Later, at home, Íso wrote a message to Eric. She explained that she was pregnant. She said that it was his child. She was sorry she hadn't told him sooner. She'd heard through Elena that he was still recovering. Perhaps that's why you don't write? I'm thinking of you. Always.

She knew of course that Eric's wife would read the message, and she knew that it might come as a shock, but she thought too that Eric and his wife had lived separate lives, and that only after Eric had the accident, when he was incapable of deciding things for himself, did his wife reclaim him.

There was no response from Eric. She did not understand. To be certain, she wrote him a regular letter and mailed it to the address he had given her when they were still close. Still close. When she said these words in her head, she was very sad.

He didn't respond.

And so she let him go.


SHE planned to have the baby at the clinic. She had a midwife, and her mother and her aunt would be present. Along with Illya. She asked Betje if she would be available if necessary. Betje was happy to say yes.

One day, a week before her delivery date, she was turning up the corridor towards the clinic's kitchen, her belly out in front of her like a ship's prow, when she saw the doctor's wife walking in the garden. She stopped and looked again, but the doctor's wife had disappeared. She waited. She put it down to a vision. Her mind was not exactly quick these days. But still, the figure had been so clear, and the angle of the jaw, and the hair. She asked Selia, one of the keepers who had known the doctor and his wife, if Doctor Mann's wife had returned to the clinic. Selia shook her head and said that she didn't think so.

The next day she was sure she heard the voice of the doctor's wife, but when she turned into the courtyard, it was empty save for the gardener, who was sweeping leaves. She asked the gardener, whose name was Felipe, if he had seen a woman pass through.

He said that the director had passed by.

Was she with someone?

He said that it was not impossible. He waved his hand in the direction of the nearby corridor.

She walked into the corridor and saw nothing. Only plants and the red baldosas of the floor, and the soft light that fell through the large windows.

Later that day, she checked the register at the front desk, searching for Susan Mann's name, but she found nothing. She counselled herself that she was being illogical.

That night she did what she had always hesitated to do: she opened her computer and typed in the search term "Doctor Eric Mann" and she put the name "Susan" after it. She found images of the doctor and his wife. He in a tuxedo and she in an evening dress. They were both smiling, her small head on his shoulder. Another of Susan in a large room with other people, holding a glass of wine, looking as if she absolutely belonged. And one of Eric alone, at a hospital somewhere in the States. And at the clinic at Ixchel, wearing a T-shirt and jeans, his long hair flowing. Eric on the motorcycle. She stared at the photos for long time. There was an article about his wife. She owned an art gallery that specialized in primitive installations. Íso wondered about the word "primitive." She went back to the photo of Doctor Mann, the one at the clinic, but it was just an image. There was no smell, no voice, nothing to touch.

The next day she came home to find her uncle Santiago standing at the counter in the tienda, talking to her mother. When Santiago saw her he hugged her and touched her stomach as if it were a delicate glass bowl and he joked about her big beauty and she asked if it was too big. Never, he said. Never, my beautiful niece. He held her hands and asked if she was worried.

Why? she asked. No.

Good, good, he said. If you worry, you come to your tío.

I'm not worried, she repeated.

That evening Íso was standing behind the counter in the tienda, selling a pack of Marlboros to an American tourist, when her water broke. She heard a pop and she felt liquid trickle down her legs, and when she looked she saw a little puddle at her feet. She excused herself and went into the back and told her mother that she was going to have the baby. Her mother flagged down a tuk-tuk, and together they rode to the clinic. Her mother kept telling the driver to slow down, and to be careful on the bumps. My daughter is having a baby, she said.

Íso had requested a small room off the main building. There was a matrimonial bed and a sink and a bathroom and there was enough room for her mother and her aunt and Illya to sit on the floor and eat and wait. And there was a window that gave out onto the garden and the pathways. It was dark. The sky was clear. When she checked in, the night nurse had asked her to sign the permiso. Íso thought it was a little silly—she worked there, didn't she?— but she signed on three separate lines, dated everything, and then declared that she was now going to have a baby.

When Francisca the midwife arrived, she pulled from her bag a stethoscope, clean towels, lotion, blankets. She laid this all out on the table beside the bed. Íso told her that she was excited and afraid.

Don't be afraid, Francisca said. She felt Íso's abdomen, moving her hands from the fundus down to her pubis. Then she touched Íso's forehead and said that she was doing well, and she sat on the floor beside Señora Perdido.

Illya arrived, carrying a basket with rice and beans and avocado and pineapple. She hugged Íso, who smelled the outside air on her skin.

Íso had observed many of the women in the village give birth. She had always been aware of their solitude and their calm natures and the fact that they didn't cry out or call for help. With each contraction she went inside herself, though she could hear Francisca singing, and her mother praying. The women sat cross-legged on the floor, and between the contractions she was aware of them eating and talking quietly together. No one paid attention to her. She was happy for the privacy.

As the contractions grew in frequency, Francisca lifted the blanket and touched her and then she took some lotion and began to massage Íso's perineum. Íso closed her eyes. She breathed quickly and then slowly, depending on her state. She saw herself as floating on water, and then she became the water and the water became her. She went under, and she rose to the surface, and again she went under. And each time she went under, she went a little deeper, so that when she looked up at the surface of the water she made out vague shapes, and dim lights, and she heard as if from a great distance her mother's voice singing. She was no longer afraid. She was quite peaceful. The final time she went under she went very deep, and as she rose she saw the surface shimmering above her, but it was quite a distance, and she was losing oxygen, and just as she felt that her lungs were finished, she broke through the surface and gasped for air and the baby was born. She did not see the baby being born, of course, but she knew, because as she sucked for air she felt an extreme euphoria, and she heard Francisca say the word bueno, and she heard the women's voices rise and fall in happiness, and in that moment she believed she had done something that no one else had ever done before, and she was amazed at herself.

She lay on the bed and turned her head towards the women sitting on the floor. Her mother was holding the baby, which was covered with a blanket. Señora Perdido removed the blanket and inspected the baby from head to toe. She touched the eyes and the nose, and the mouth, which worked vigorously. She put her finger inside the baby's mouth and felt the palate. She moved the baby's arms back and forth. She touched between its legs and said that it was a girl. Then she handed the baby to Illya, who kissed the baby's head. The women dressed the girl in a striped blue top and a cortez. Francisca told Íso that it was time to birth the placenta. She closed her eyes and suffered some more birth pangs, and as she did so she wondered if she was doing everything in the correct manner. But Francisca did not say anything other than bueno and so Íso believed that everything had been good. Francisca left and returned with atole and fresh tortillas. Íso ate and she drank tea. She watched the women pass the baby between them. And then Illya stood and handed the baby to Íso, and she took her and held her.

At night, alone with the baby, she was fierce with love. The birth was beautiful. The baby was beautiful. The fingernails and the toe-nails and the arches of the feet and the heart beating through the fontanelle. All of this. And the knuckles. And the fists clenching and unclenching. The generous mouth. Íso had breastfed imme-diately, and even though she had no milk yet, the baby had latched well. Her family and Illya and Francisca had stayed late and then finally left to get some sleep. They would return for her in the morning. She talked to the baby. She told her that she was hand-some and strong, and look at her eyes, and she had such hair, and wasn't she lucky, and she said that she would have the perfect name, and wasn't she guapa, and didn't she have the longest fingers and such big feet.

She fell asleep and woke to touch the sleeping child, and she fell asleep again.

A nurse came in and woke her and said that she would take the baby for a bath. Íso didn't know the nurse, though she thought she should, and she asked the nurse if she couldn't wait until morning and then she, Íso, would bath the baby. She said that she loved the smell of a newborn, and she dipped her head and smelled the child, as if to prove her words. But she was very happy and her hormones were wild and she was very proud and because of this her mind was not clear, and so she kissed the baby's head and let her go. She told the nurse to come straight back after the bath. The sun was about to rise. She saw the light at the edge of the volcano, which was visible from the large window in her room. The line of the volcano's backside was perfectly straight, as if drawn by a giant with an enormous ruler. It was black and straight save for a single tree that towered over all the others. A tree with a large canopy.

She fell asleep, and woke to the noise of birds in the garden. The sun was bright. It was morning. She thought immediately of her baby. She sat up. Her breasts hurt. She called out. No one came. She called again, a little louder this time, but still in a natural voice because she didn't want to seem impractical. The nurse must have put the baby in the nursery. She got up and slipped into a robe. She felt a little pain, but she could walk without difficulty. In the hallway, it was hushed. Still early. The baldosas were smooth and cool on her feet as she moved through the corridor to the nursery.

There was no one on duty.

The nursery was dark and empty.

She stood in the dimness.

She had many thoughts, and some of the thoughts were panicky, but she did not allow the bad thoughts to stay with her. There would be a practical explanation. The baby was being admired by the keepers who had just arrived. The baby was being held because it was fussy. She left the nursery and returned to her room. It was empty. The garden beyond the window was bluish grey in the new light. A hummingbird floated above a bird of paradise. She saw the bird and she saw the flower and she thought that everything must be normal. It was good.

She dressed, and even as she dressed she was aware that she was doing something wrong. She put on her underwear and she slipped her dress over her head and as it fell to her knees she felt the lightness of the material against her skin. Everything was exaggerated. The silence of the room, the fall of the cloth over her head, the whisper of her feet going into her sandals, her thin and quick breathing. She tried to remember the nurse. A silver bracelet on her left wrist. Voice low. Soft and convincing. Just a quick bath. She shook her head now and felt her throat close. All this wasted movement. But she thought that if she was dressed and prepared for her baby, then she would be shown the place where the baby lay, and she would pick the baby up and everything would be normal. There was an explanation.

Her hands were shaking, and she heard someone whimpering, and she knew that the noise was coming from her own mouth. She stepped out into the hallway. A keeper passed by. Have you seen my baby? she asked. The keeper looked at her and shook her head, and then walked on. She moved in the opposite direction of the keeper, towards the entrance of the clinic. There were tall flowering plants in large clay pots standing sentinel beside the main doors, and though she had seen these plants and clay pots many times before, she had never noticed their elegance and their colour and their size. Like guardians flanking the entrance. A nurse was sitting at the main desk. She told the nurse that she was looking for her baby. It was with me last night, and then a woman came, a nurse, and she took it, and she didn't bring it back. She was speaking Spanish but the nurse didn't understand, so she said in English, My baby. It's gone.

The nurse stood and came around the desk and asked her name. She had a Dutch accent.

Íso. It's Íso.

And the baby's name? the nurse asked.

No name. Not yet.

The nurse guided her to a cane chair and told her to sit. She went back to the desk and picked up the phone. Íso watched her. She saw her speaking but she could not hear the words. The nurse hung up and came back towards Íso, holding a glass of water.

Íso took it and drank. Is it coming? she asked.

The nurse said that the director would come soon.

No, Íso said. Not the director. My baby.

The nurse held her hand. She must have thought Íso was crazy, because she stroked Íso's head and said that everything would be fine. Don't worry, she said. You're upset.

The director did not come. Íso waited, and the longer she waited the more aware she became of the tall plants in the clay pots, and she imagined that the plants were growing right before her eyes. The nurse was sitting again behind the front desk.

She said to the nurse, It's gone. My baby.

That's ridiculous, the nurse said. Babies don't just walk away. Is it a girl?

Íso nodded.

She's here somewhere, the nurse said and smiled, and Íso smiled back, because what else was she to do. She didn't want to be ridiculous.

Her hands were shaking. Her legs. And still she sat, not moving. Which was wrong. She sat and thought of all the wrong things. She thought of her hunger and she thought of the birth and she thought of her mother, who would be at home. She thought about simple things, like the colours of the flowers in the pots, and the types of flowers, and then she stopped and was appalled by her thoughts. But as soon as she thought about the baby she couldn't breathe and she felt faint and her heart went desolate, and none of this was good. She had to stay alert and strong. But still, the baby. And so she stood and began to walk back along the corridor towards the garden. And then she ran, and then she walked because it seemed wrong to run, and then she ran again because time was crucial. The Dutch nurse called out in her flat voice, but she ignored the nurse, who knew nothing and only took directions from the director.

Íso stepped into the garden and went to the first woman she saw and she asked, Have you seen my baby? It was early and the woman was alone and drinking her morning tea. She looked up and shook her head. It was all so disconcerting. For the woman. For Íso. She began to knock on doors to the rooms. She called out. Some women tried to console her. Others ignored her. All saw her as deranged. Even the keepers she came upon shied away. She found herself in the pool area, fearing that her baby had been drowned. But how? And for what reason?

And this is where Elena found her, at the edge of the pool, staring down into the water. She took Íso by the arm and said, Come. Come.

My baby, Íso said. She's gone.

They walked together back down the corridor towards the room in which Íso had birthed the baby and then fed the baby and then slept, holding the baby. As they walked, hand in hand, Íso began to feel calmer, and she realized that the baby was of course back in the room. Here she'd been running all over looking for a baby that was where it was supposed to be. They entered the room, Elena first. Íso followed. The room was empty.

She's not here, Íso said.

Elena took her by the shoulders and looked into her face and said, She is gone.

Gone?

Yes.

She's dead?

No, Íso, no. She's safe. Elena guided Íso to a chair. Sit, she said.

I won't sit, Íso cried.

You must. You'll faint otherwise.

But where? she whispered. Where has she gone?

Elena touched her shoulder.

Íso pulled back. Where? she said again.

To Doctor Mann and his wife.

They were here? In this place? Doctor Mann is here?

His wife was here. She has the baby.

No. No. The baby is mine.

As she is the doctor's, Elena said. You signed the papers. You released the baby.

The papers? I didn't know. I didn't know. What are you saying? She was shouting now.

You signed the papers, Elena said again. The baby is gone.

There was the sound of a wail and it was so distant and so eerie that it frightened Íso, and she covered her ears and fell to her knees in order not to hear that horrible cry, but still it came and came and came, and then someone was lifting her and carrying her, and she was laid on her bed and a doctor appeared—Betje, it was—and Betje held up a syringe and said it was for calming down, and she felt the needle in her thigh, and then she felt nothing.

In the early days, just after her baby was taken, Íso went to the police station in her village and she spoke with one of the officers.

She sat for a long time in the anteroom and when she was called into the inner office she explained her situation. The officer was a short man in a tight-fitting uniform. He was patient, but he seemed bored. He explained that there was little to be done. It was out of his hands. And he raised the hands he had just referred to and held them palms up towards the ceiling, as if hoping that something of value might fall down and benefit him. Íso understood that this was a plea for money, and she understood that the bribe might produce nothing. Her breasts were leaking, even though she had expressed milk that morning, and she was aware that the officer had noticed the wet spots on her shirt. Respectfully, he made every obvious effort not to look at her chest.

She spoke to a lawyer, who advised her to hire an American lawyer. He said that he had no power over these kinds of things. It was out of his hands. He too made a gesture, and this gesture seemed to indicate the senselessness of the world. She saw many different officials. Some were greedy and wanted money for nothing, others saw her as a fool who had tumbled into a place of her own deserving, and one man treated her as a puta. He was interested in her.

She rode the bus to the city and went to the US embassy and she inquired into the legal rights she had. She was told that even if the child was hers, she would have to go to the place of residence of the father and press charges against him. Even so, she might not gain anything. She had signed the papers allowing the child to be taken. The father had his rights as well.

~~~~~

IN the weeks that followed the disappearance of Íso's baby, there were rumours of a change of policy at the clinic: there would be no more contract births. But then the rumours subsided and everything continued as usual. Elena ruled in the same manner, with a feigned benevolence. A fresh deluge of barren women arrived fortnightly to take the waters. The keepers cared for their charges. The doctors in the outpatient clinic saw children with earaches and they saw campesinos with broken limbs. A new group of foreign doctors and nurses arrived—young and idealistic and brimming with notions of charity and goodwill. The salaries of the local workers remained the same. The clinic founder, Doctor August, grew richer.

Íso wrote Doctor Mann and his wife messages that begged for an explanation and a reply. No response came. She became wild and inconsolable. She slept and woke and her mother tended to her, and then she slept some more because she could not bear being awake. Eventually, she grew quiet and found a place where she might put the child. In her heart. She had no photographs, just a memory of that first night, holding her baby and then feeding her, and then sleeping side by side. It was her own mother who had told her that she must decide to be at peace. The baby was alive. The baby was taken care of. The baby was with the father.

She no longer worked at the clinic. She took care of her mother's tienda. In the evenings, sometimes, when she heard the sound of a Honda motorcycle approaching, she looked up as if expecting the miraculous, but then the motorcycle passed on and she returned to her books. She was now reading textbooks, biology and chemistry. She had hired a tutor and would reapply soon for medical school at a university in the city. She had no doubts that she would be accepted.

Six weeks after the child was taken, Elena contacted her and asked her to come by for a talk. It is important, she said.

On the day of their meeting, Íso dressed in jeans and flat shoes and a white blouse and she pulled her hair back in a ponytail. She walked to the clinic, following the road that ran alongside the lake. Women were washing clothes along the shore. Children swam. The many boats that crossed the lake every day were like small white warnings against the high waves. It was very windy, and she was grateful that her hair was not loose. She wanted to appear composed and calm when she met Elena.

She had not been back to the clinic since the day after the birth, when her mother had arrived to take her home. And so now, as she stepped into the silence of the entrance and walked past the tall plants that sat like guardians in their large clay pots, she found it difficult to breathe. She announced herself and sat in a chair that looked out over the inner courtyard. A woman, foreign, sat barefoot amongst the ferns. She was blonde and thin, as they most often were, and she was reading. She looked up and noticed Íso and smiled. Íso smiled back and bowed her head. It was a habit she had not yet forgotten.

Elena, when she appeared, seemed younger and more beautiful, and Íso saw that she had cut her hair. She rose. She stepped forward. Elena gestured that she should come into her office.

When they were seated—Elena behind her desk, Íso on a

couch that was low to the ground—Elena said that they would not stoop to small talk. You have many questions, and I will have some answers, but you won't like or understand my answers. And so it would be useless to ask the questions.

Íso said that perhaps the questions were useless to Elena, but for her they were essential. She asked if the first offer for the child had come from the doctor and his wife.

No, that was from Odette. The doctor and his wife only learned of the child later. You wrote to them, yes?

But you told me to write. They didn't know? Before I wrote?

No.

Íso bowed her head and breathed. Then she looked up and said, Susan was here. I saw her, didn't I? In the garden. You planned this together.

There was no plan. Life is not that organized. The world is round. Things sometimes just happen.

But the papers I signed. You organized that. And tricked me.

Elena waved a hand. Everyone must sign papers. That is the rule. You can see it as a trick if it makes you feel better.

Were you paid to help steal the child?

It was not a theft.

How much were you paid? Íso asked.

Elena shook her head. Would it make a difference if it was a lot? Or a little?

However much, it was enough.

Would you have wanted that the baby be cut in half?

She was mine.

And she was the doctor's. This was not my decision. Ten thousand dollars will come to you, she said. It is from Doctor Mann and his wife. It is for your trouble.

I don't want it, Íso said.

Then I will give it to your mother, who will keep it for you.

Like me, she doesn't want it.

Don't be so sure what someone else wants or doesn't want.

It is money full of greed and sin, Íso said.

It is just money, Elena said. And money is useful. For university, for helping your mother, for living. You think that if you don't take the money, then you can alter what has happened. And that if you do take the money, then you are agreeing to a covenant. You agreed long ago. When you first met Doctor Mann and fell in love, you agreed to something. You acted foolishly, or perhaps wisely, or perhaps you acted and there was not wisdom or foolishness, just a simple choice. But you did choose, and your life moved along, as did Doctor Mann's. You knew he was married, but still you chose him. You knew he was from elsewhere, but still you chose him. You wanted to believe you were special. Did he promise you anything? Did he say that he would be with you forever? You are alone, Íso. Just you. Even if he had been from here, and his name had been José or Carlos or Roberto, you would still be on your own. In the end you have only Íso. That is all. You might learn that eventually, or you might never learn that. Perhaps those who never learn this fact are the most fortunate. They are naive but at peace. The lucky ones. You, Íso, are not so lucky. But you are still young, and you are intelligent, and you have many years in front of you.

I didn't choose to be without my child, Íso said. You have children.

I do.

And so you're not alone.

You're being too plain in your interpretation.

Do you love your children? Íso asked.

Of course.

And what would you do if you lost a child?

I would think I was going to die, Elena said. But I wouldn't. I learned long ago that I must give up my child. In my head. Give the child to the earth, to God, to the world, to death, to the possibility of death, to the possibility of disease, and in doing so I became at peace. Because I had let my child go. And in letting the child go I became colder, more distant, and more at peace. But I still loved the child, don't be wrong. As you love your child. I am sorry.

SHE did not speak to her mother about the offer of money. She had told Elena no, but Elena had said that the money would still be available should Íso change her mind. It will not run away, Elena said.

And so the idea of the money sat inside her like the seed from a poisonous plant. And she decided that there would be only one reason to take it, and having decided this, she returned to Elena and said that she was ready. For several months the money rested in her account in the small bank that bordered the central square near the market. She had never had so much, and she knew that her mother had never had so much. She was restless. She could not sleep. She was impatient with her life and with her mother and with the people who came into the tienda to buy butter or cheese or rolled oats. Why eat butter when there is a baby out there without a mother? The seed inside her grew and one day she told her mother that she could no longer wait for her permission papers to be processed. She said that she would be leaving the following week. Her plans were set.

Her mother touched Íso's head and said that she was surprised Íso had not gone sooner. If you must go, she said, then you will go with my blessing.

# 6.

IN HER BACKPACK SHE HAD EXTRA UNDERWEAR AND SOCKS and a sweater, and she had a flashlight, her toothbrush and toothpaste, a New Testament from her mother, maps of Mexico and the United States, and she had a bottle of water and two oranges and tortillas and beans to eat on the road. She had five thousand US dollars in an envelope, which was for the man, and she had one thousand dollars wrapped in cellophane and taped to her waist. She had left the remainder with her mother. She wore around her neck the carving that Santiago had given her. She had no identification, and everything that was true about her—anything that could be known—was inside her own head. She wore dark runners and dark jeans and a dark T-shirt because this is what was advised. The T-shirt was too large but she preferred this because she didn't want to reveal so easily that she was a woman. She wore a Giants cap, and she tucked her hair up beneath the cap so that from a distance she might appear to be a boy.

They were eight, and this included the guide, who called himself Marcos. He was a big man with a head like a hammer, very flat, and when he spoke it was so softly that you had to lean in to understand what he wanted to say. There was a tattoo of Jesus on his left forearm, and the words "Es mi guia," and in the days to come he would reveal that he had spent ten years in prison and during that time he had found the Lord and now it was his duty to help those who were lost. He wore a chain with a wooden cross. He was not the man who took the money. This was a man who sat in the passenger seat of the van and said nothing, except when he hopped out at the edge of the city, his pockets full, and called out, Good luck and pray that you do not see me again. And he was gone, the man with no name.

Most of them were young, sixteen to twenty, though there was one boy, a mere child, who sat in the back seat beside Íso.

He said his name and he said that his mother was in Houston. He said it as if it was a memorized word, a word that meant nothing to him, some distant dot in a great country, whispered in his ear by a brother or a mother or a father. He took her hand. She allowed this and then thought better of it and pulled it away. He reached for it again, searching, and found her and held on tightly.

My name's Gabriel, he said. And you?

She didn't answer.

Will you be my friend? the boy asked. The others in the van were ignoring him.

No, she said. Find someone else. But in speaking to him she realized that she had opened the door into which he would stick his head. Short hair, big ears, small teeth. She pulled her hand away and turned towards the window.

The boy sighed and hiccupped and eventually fell asleep against her shoulder. His head was tiny and very light. His wrists were thin. He carried nothing. When he woke, the morning had almost arrived. The edges of the mountains were black against the sky, and then the sun appeared, and she saw the others in the van. She was the only girl.

They stopped at a roadside restaurant and Marcos said that they weren't to talk to anyone. Use the bathroom and come back to the van. If you buy food, get it at the cantina. Maria will serve you.

She went to the women's washroom and Gabriel followed her.

Go piss like a boy, she said, and pushed him towards the men's bathroom. When she came out he was still standing there.

Did you go? she asked.

He shook his head. She motioned to the bathroom door, and after he entered she closed the door and stood guard. He came out grinning. On their way back to the van he manoeuvred through the tables and held out his palm for money or food, and when he climbed into the van he had a little of both. They shared her tortillas and beans and drank her water, and they ate the sweet bun he was given. One of the young men had purchased potato tamales and he ate these from a Styrofoam container and the smell filled the van and made her hungry. She chewed slowly at her tortilla.

Gabriel nudged her and lifted his T-shirt and showed her a piece of paper pinned to the underside.

She shook her head.

He worked for a long time at the safety pin and finally released the paper and pushed it at her.

She shook her head again.

He opened the paper and held it up for her to read.

She took it. It was a note, written in English, introducing the boy, who was seven and whose mother, Beatrice, lived in Houston. An address was given. The final line said, Much thank you to take my son, Gabriel. God bless.

She read it twice and then pushed it back at him.

He put it in his pants pocket.

Do you have money? she asked.

He shook his head.

Nothing?

He shook his head.

Who wrote the note? she asked.

My father.

Your father, she said.

Yes.

Your father's crazy.

His eyes were dark and empty. He nodded, willing to accept whatever she said.

~~~~

SHE had said goodbye to Illya during her last week at home. They walked arm in arm through the streets and Íso told Illya that she was leaving to find her baby.

To the States?

Yes.

Alone?

Yes.

His wife will fight you. You know that.

Yes.

Do you have a plan?

I will go to their city, and I will find them, and I will take the baby.

That's not a plan.

It's all I have.

If you're caught, you'll be deported. Without the baby.

I won't be caught.

Oh, Íso. Do you have enough money?

The money I was paid for the baby. It is enough.

Does your mother know?

Yes, she agrees.

There are other ways. Legal ways. You could find a lawyer.

Íso shook her head. No, she said.

They stood in the street, facing each other. Illya hugged Íso. Every day I'll think of you, she whispered. Be careful. It will be dangerous.

I'm smart, Íso said. I'm strong.

Illya hugged her again.

Her mother, in order to prepare Íso, had laid out maps of Mexico and the United States on the small table in the cocina in the evenings and showed her the route that she might take. Her mother paid particular attention to the map of the United States. She circled cities such as San Antonio and Houston and San Francisco. She said that she had names of people in San Francisco, though it had been years and she didn't know if her old friends still lived there, or if they were still alive. But they must be, she said. I'm still alive. She drew a line from the Mexican border up to the city of Saint Falls, where Doctor Mann lived. It was a long distance, and as she pushed her yellow marker along the interstates and roads that climbed up to that distant city, she shook her head and said, It is far. You'll take the bus, she said. She told Íso that if she was stopped by the border patrol, or if she was caught, she should say that she had a baby in the country. And a husband.

Íso set her mother up with a messaging account so that they could communicate. She took her to a Tigo shop and they sat beside each other and Íso taught her mother how to find her account and how to send messages. One evening they sat in the dim light of the shop and they sent messages back and forth to each other, laughing together, her mother awkward with the technology, but finally understanding.

After, they walked home arm in arm, past the women cutting fruit, and past the tortilla stands, and past a barbershop where through a single door they saw men and boys waiting solemnly in plastic chairs, and on through the main square, where, on the basketball court, a game was taking place. They stood and watched for a while. One of the teams had a very tall white man who was quite slow and couldn't keep up, but he scored easily. Íso said that Doctor Mann had played basketball here sometimes. She had watched him. He was very quick, she said. Her mother was quiet. They sat on a low wall of stone behind one of the baskets, their arms entwined. The crowd watching the game did not cheer or make any noise, and so the only sounds were those of sneakers on the concrete, and the ball bouncing, and the occasional shout from one of the players, and the referee's whistle.

They stood finally and walked on, down the road towards the tienda.

That night Íso coloured her mother's hair. She put on rubber gloves and mixed the solution and, using the long end of the comb, pulled her mother's hair back in layers and carefully brushed in the solution. Always when she did this, she was aware of how vulnerable her mother was. Her mother's scalp. Her mother's eyebrows. The lines on her mother's forehead. Her closed eyes.

There, she said when she was finished. Until next time.

Her last night at home, she had heard her mother crying. Very softly. She wanted to speak to her mother then, or to hold her, but she did not let her mother know that she was awake. If her mother had wanted to let Íso know that she was sad, she would have cried during the day. After, when her mother had finished crying and appeared to be sleeping again, Íso put her hand on her mother's back and held it there until she too fell asleep.

~~~~~

AT the Mexican border they crossed the Suchiate by raft into Talisman. A flat wooden vessel that held nine of them. A cable extended from one bank to the other. The pilot was a young man named Moises and he said that he was happy to offer them a ride on his zip line. He grinned. I'm your driver, he said, and here is your private boat. He told them to sit or stand, it was their choice, but not to fall into the water because there were alligators, and when he said this he looked at Gabriel and he winked. Mexican police stood with rifles on the bridge above them, but they simply watched, and at one point Moises saluted the police and called out a good day. They nodded solemnly, as if this undertaking on the river below was part of a larger scheme over which they had no control. Or over which they had ultimate control. Or perhaps they were paid. Marcos too seemed indifferent to the presence of the police. On the other side, they clambered up the bank, and Marcos led them through small streets and past a market where all manner of goods were sold, melons and tomatoes and butchered chickens and shoes and plastic balls of all colours, one of which the boy wanted.

When we arrive, she said.

Watermelon, he said, and she took his hand and pulled him along. A child, not more than six, walked parallel to their group, carrying a bag of T-shirts and sweaters, naming the prices for such fine ware. He also claimed to have candles, hats, cigarettes, small candies, peanuts. All this was available. And then he disappeared.

Marcos took them deep into the city, finally stopping at a building painted the colour of a ripe papaya. He entered a dark doorway. They leaned against the wall out of the sun and waited. On the street a dog walked along the shaded side and as it approached it gave them a wide berth and moved sideways, its rear end twisted and hollowed. A wedding party passed, the bride and groom standing in the back of a pickup, an old man next to them playing trumpet. When the din and excitement was gone, a single balloon lay in the street. The boy ran and picked it up and played in the shade of the building, talking to himself.

Two hours later a van pulled up, the same one they had left before crossing the Suchiate. A woman climbed out and entered the dark doorway and a while later Marcos reappeared and gestured at the van. Your private beast, he said. Climb aboard. And he laughed.

They drove for three days, stopping whenever Marcos grew tired, through Chiapas and Oaxaca and Mexico City and San Luis Potosí, up into Nuevo León. In the smaller towns they stopped in the central square and filled their water bottles using the spigots where women washed laundry. Women dressed in the cloth of their tribe, speaking languages she had never heard. She learned the boys' names. They learned hers. She did not speak out of turn, and when it was required, she spoke softly and with few words. She was aware that these boys were farmers' sons, and that they were sons of coffee pickers, and that they were very poor. She was aware of her own status—the fact that she knew English, and that she had some sense of where they were headed, and that her experience with the American students at her school in Panajachel could only benefit her. These were the facts, and she kept these facts in her head.

One of the boys, Benito, was interested in her and he kept his eye on her, and after one of the gas station stops, during which she bought tamales for herself and Gabriel, Benito climbed into the back of the van beside her. She placed the boy between herself and Benito, and she turned towards the window. She fell asleep and woke to discover Benito's hand between her legs. She exhaled with a hiss and pushed him away. Bastard, she said.

He grinned, his teeth shining in the darkness. He said he was horny and she too must be horny, so young and so beautiful, and if she wanted help, he would do so. Understand? he asked.

She carried, in the front pocket of her jeans, a knife that her tío had given her. She reached for it now and held it up for Benito to see and she said, If you touch me or the boy, I'll kill you.

The boy was sleeping and the others were sleeping and Marcos was singing along to a religious song on the radio, and so no one heard. She could smell Benito. She did not know if he believed her and so she said again, I'll kill you. The knife was in her fist and her fist lay on her thigh and her body shook, but not her voice. Go, she said, and he shrugged and climbed back to his spot in the middle of the van.

She sat without sleeping and when she found that her head was falling into her chest she rubbed her eyes and looked out into the darkness and tried to sing along with the voices on the radio and then she slept and woke, aware that she had slept, and she was dismayed.

At night, from then on, she held the knife in her fist as she slept. And during the day she avoided Benito. He still watched her and he watched the boy, as if jealous of the boy's position. She and the boy had taken to eating together, drinking together, sleeping together, and when the van stopped and she climbed down to go to the bathroom in the bush, he followed her and they pissed together. Don't look, she said, squatting, and he turned away and then turned back to watch her. Holding his little beak. She made a shooing motion with her hand and he grinned. She knew that she was in less danger because of Gabriel. It was much easier to attack a girl who was alone than a girl with a seven-year-old child. And so she slept with Gabriel in her arms, his small head pressed against her stomach.

THEY crossed the Rio Grande at night just north of Piedras Negras. Marcos did not go with them. He pointed across the river and said, Por ahí. On the other side there were lights and vehicles and men, and all around them in the water there were other people, and the most amazing part was the silence, for no one spoke. Just the splashing and the breathing and the occasional gasp, and then more silence, save for the hum of truck engines on the other side. Gabriel held her pack and clung to her as she lay across a rubber tube and kicked with her feet. His little arms around her neck. Their group formed a V in the water, with Benito at the head of the V. A body floated past her, face down, long dark hair spread out. She pushed the body away and kept kicking. She took water into her mouth. Swallowed it. Gasped and sputtered. Gabriel said her name. She told him to be quiet. And then beneath her bare feet she felt mud and the bank and she was clambering up from the water to the land. She took Gabriel's hand and plucked him upwards, trailing Benito's broad back. He was bent over and following the bank of river. And then a light came on and the world was brightly lit and a voice called out.

They ran. There were shouts and lights and people running and she took Gabriel into her arms and she ran towards the darkness but the darkness moved farther away and so she ran back and then forwards and back again until finally she was once again in the darkness and she ran in that darkness like the fastest runner and when she had finished running she was still holding Gabriel and it was still dark. Far behind her she saw the lights and she saw men and she saw the men corralling other men and boys and girls, and then she turned and ran with the darkness.

In the cold of the morning she saw the pink light in the sky and she saw the cacti take shape and she saw the wide sky and a bird circling high above. She had covered Gabriel with a sweater from her pack and she had put on his runners and she had cleaned her own feet of thorns and scrapes and put on her own shoes, and so she sat, watching the sunrise, waiting for the boy to wake.

She stood and turned a full circle, looking out into that space where the land and the sky met. She walked one hundred steps in one direction and then returned. One hundred steps in the opposite direction and returned. The river was gone. The people were gone. She looked for footprints that might indicate where they had come from. Nothing. The land was hard and dry. They had two small bottles of water. No food. One hat. An extra sweater. Shoes. When the boy woke she let him drink. He drank and drank and in drinking so much he spilled water onto the ground. She took the bottle and screwed on the lid and said, Enough.

Are we lost? the boy asked.

She shook her head.

Will we go to my mother now?

She looked at him. His small head. Small hands. She said, Yes, we'll go.

She stood and took a T-shirt from her pack and tied it around his head. Little gangster, she said.

He laughed.

It was still early morning, and with the sun on her right she began to walk. The boy was distracted by lizards and flowers and bugs. This made him happy and so she let him be and in this way their progress was slow. She drank from her water, a small taste. It was already warm and sour. She told the boy that they would get one drink every hour.

He asked how she would know an hour without a watch to tell time.

The time, it's in my head, she said, and she touched her forehead.

What time is it now? he asked.

Nine o'clock.

I'm hungry, he said.

We'll eat when we arrive.

When will we arrive?

Soon.

At what time? He reached up and touched her forehead.

Very soon.

When?

She did not answer.

When the sun was at its highest they sat behind a cactus, seeking shade. Her shoulders were exposed but her head was shaded and the boy sat before her using her body as shade. They drank. And then drank some more. She took the empty bottle and threw it out onto the floor of the desert. It lay there.

That night she heard animals calling and talking and she heard something small moving across the nearby ground. She sat up and waited and watched. The moon was thin and the night was dark. There were stars and the stars were the same ones she knew from her home, but she didn't know their names or how they worked. A plane passed high overhead, lights blinking. Just before the sun rose it was very cold and she was shivering and her fingers were numb and her feet were numb. She blew breath onto her hands and she beat her hands against her legs. She rubbed her legs until her palms and legs were warm again, and she fell asleep sitting up. She woke to discover the boy drinking the last of the water.

She took the bottle and held it up to discover its emptiness, and then she threw the bottle out into the desert and she turned to the boy and hit him across the head.

He began to cry.

Stupid, she said. Where do you think we'll get more water? Where? From a lake? From a river? Or the tienda over there? She pointed out into the desert and the boy looked, as if expecting a little store to pop up.

She stood and went to the bottle and picked it up and put it in her pack. She began to walk. When she looked back the boy was sitting as she had left him. She waited, and finally the boy stood and followed her.

They walked until the boy sat down. He said that he was thirsty and that his legs wouldn't move. She stood over him. His mouth was open and she saw his tongue and it was black. She squatted and told him to climb onto her back. He did so and put his arms around her neck and she rose and though the weight of the boy was not much at all she stumbled slightly and then found her balance and began to walk. Her arms reached behind her in order to hold the boy. Her arms grew tired and her legs were failing but still she walked. The boy was quiet. She said his name. He did not answer. She asked if he was sleeping. Nothing. Still, she talked to him. She told him that there was a mountain in the distance and there would be trees at the base of the mountain, and when they reached the trees there would be shade and there would be a stream or even a river. She said, We'll drink the water from the river and we'll swim. We'll splash in the water and put our heads under the water. The boy did not answer and she stopped talking because it made her thirsty.

When the sun was at its highest she laid the boy down beside a cactus and she crouched over him to protect him. He'd lost the

T-shirt she'd put on his head. He looked up at her and smiled
and then closed his eyes. She closed her own eyes and when she
opened them she saw before her an iguana. The iguana was the
colour of the ground and at first she imagined she was dreaming
but then its tail moved and she knew she was not alone. She took
her knife from her pocket and stood. The iguana moved sideways. Its tongue darted. She took a step forwards and the iguana
moved backwards. She held the knife over her head and threw it.
The knife bounced off the ground and skidded away. The iguana
blinked and skittered off beneath some low-lying plants. She
chased the iguana through the desert and finally killed it with a
small rock that was thrown from a distance. A lucky throw, one
she could never repeat. She carried the iguana back to where the
boy lay and she found her knife and she slit the yellow belly of
the iguana and she bent to lick at the blood and the liquid that
spilled out. There was little meat and it was tough and raw, but it
produced in her mouth a liquid of sorts, and she discovered that
if she sucked slowly at the meat, her mouth produced saliva and
she swallowed the saliva. She held a piece of the iguana before
the boy's mouth, rubbing his lips, and his black tongue came out
briefly but he didn't eat or chew or take anything into his mouth.
She finished off the iguana, leaving only the tail and the shell of
it on the desert floor. Then she picked up the boy and once again
began to walk.

Evening found them no closer to the mountain—it seemed
instead that the mountain was moving away from them. They slept
curled into each other and she felt the boy's chest move in and out

and she lay awake for a long time, wondering if he would die, and then she fell asleep.

In the morning when she woke she knew that he was dead. She said his name and she touched him and then she drew away and said his name again and when he did not respond she stood and looked down at him.

She looked out over the landscape and she looked down at the boy and then she picked him up and put him on her back and she started to walk. He was heavier now and she had a hard time holding him up, and finally she lowered him to the ground and said, I cannot.

She waited and watched and then she rose and walked the area and found a low-lying spot, where she fell to her knees and hollowed out space for his body. The ground was softer here and as she dug lower she discovered that her hands were damp. She dug deeper. The ground was wet and if she waited the smallest amount of moisture rose to the surface. She lowered her head into the depression and put her tongue to the sand. Felt the dampness. Her face experienced the coolness of the sand and her mouth was relieved. She went back to where the boy lay and she removed his T-shirt. She pulled it off his body carefully, lifting him from behind and scrolling the shirt up his back and then over his head. And finally off his arms. She lowered the boy back onto the sand and took the T-shirt and went over to the depression she had dug. There was a quarter inch of water in the hole. She soaked up the water with the boy's shirt and then raised it to her mouth and sucked on the shirt. It was water. There was sand as well, but it was water. Over the next several hours she repeated this many times, and each time as she waited for the water to appear she took the damp shirt and tied it around her head and she sucked on a corner of the T-shirt and moved her tongue around inside her mouth. When she had had her fill of water she began to twist the T-shirt over the opening of the water bottle, and in this manner she managed to put an inch of water into the bottle. She screwed on the lid. Put the bottle inside her pack.

She went back to the boy and picked him up under his arms and dragged him towards the depression. She rolled his body down into the hole and when she looked down at him he was very small. She kneeled there and dug in his pockets and found the slip of paper with his mother's name and address on it. She put this into her own pocket. She removed one of his runners and set it aside. Then she scraped at the sand with her fingers and hands and began to cover him. She covered his face at the very last. She touched his face and his eyes and his mouth and she talked to him. She said she was sorry for hitting him, and she was sorry for not being kinder, and she was sorry that she had not saved him. She thought she might be crying but there were no tears and she realized that she had very little moisture left in her own body. This frightened and alarmed her. She took the damp T-shirt and laid it over his face and then she pushed the sand towards where his head was and when she was done he was no longer visible. She stood and found a small rock and placed it on top of the grave. Then she picked up his shoe, put it into her pack, and began to walk.

~~~~~

ISABELLA and Jack Farago owned a small ranch thirty miles east of Marfa, Texas. Isabella was Mexican, Jack American, and they'd lived together going on almost twelve years now after meeting at the Sandhills Rodeo. Isabella was driving back from her sister's place in Piedras Negras when she saw a boy kneeling beside the road. She slowed and stopped and got out and stood by her door and called out. The boy didn't raise his head or say anything. He was holding a shoe in his hand and he lifted it now and held it up for Isabella to see, and then a noise came from his mouth and she realized that this was a girl kneeling before her.

In the pickup, she gave the girl water but she couldn't drink properly, and so Isabella held the bottle for her and dribbled a little water onto her mouth and lips. The girl's tongue came out and it was thick and swollen and black and Isabella said, Jesus.

Here, she said, and she took a bandana from her pocket and soaked it with water and pressed the bandana against the girl's mouth and face. Her eyes were swollen nearly shut. The shoe she had held up was still clutched in one hand. It was a sneaker, too small for the girl's feet. The girl sucked on the rag and then sucked some more. Then she drank straight from the bottle and immediately bent forward and retched. A thin line of bile trickled between her feet.

Slow down, Isabella said. She touched the girl's back. Started the pickup and pulled out on the highway.

At the house she walked her into the bathroom and she ran a cool bath and told the girl to remove her clothes. The girl seemed embarrassed and so Isabella showed her how to turn the water off.

She showed her how to wet the washcloth and suck at it slowly, so as not to make herself sick. She went into her own bedroom and found jeans and a T-shirt from when she was younger and thinner. She found a pair of underwear. She opened the bathroom door a crack and called out, Is it good? There was no answer, but she heard the water splash. She laid the clothes inside the bathroom door and told the girl to use them.

She made the girl a fruit shake and she fried some rice and beans and she set the table and then sat down and waited. When the girl appeared Isabella told her to sit, and to eat. And drink. The girl looked about and asked, Where is the shoe?

Isabella pointed at the doorway. Beside your bag, she said. It's safe.

The girl looked in order to verify this, and then sat down and studied the food. She didn't touch anything for the longest time. She just stared. Then she picked up the glass and drank a little of the fruit shake and put the glass down. She picked up the fork and took a small amount of beans. She had a hard time chewing. She swallowed and put the fork down. It's very good, she said.

Take your time, Isabella said.

The girl ate some more. The girl drank a little. There was a glass of ice water, and the girl drank from this as well.

Isabella watched. She said, finally, What's your name?

My name is Íso Perdido.

I'm Isabella.

The girl looked up and said, Much pleasure.

Where are you from? Isabella asked.

The girl looked around and then looked at Isabella and told her. Isabella nodded. You came alone? she asked.

The girl bowed her head and then nodded.

Do you have papers? A permit?

I have nothing.

Isabella sighed. Then she told the girl that she was dehydrated and she would have to rest and drink water slowly, but by the morning she would feel better. She said that her husband, Jack, would be home soon. Don't be frightened by him, she said. He's an American who thinks immigration should have been stopped after his own family arrived here. We met at a rodeo. He was a bull rider and I was a Mexican immigrant working the hot dog stand. To Jack's way of thinking, there are always exceptions to rules. He's got a big heart.

The girl listened and nodded and said, The food is delicious. Thank you.

After, Isabella showed her a small room with a single bed and she lay down and promptly slept. When she woke she heard the voices of a man and a woman and they were speaking English and Spanish. The English voice was loud and this was the man. And then Isabella spoke and the girl heard her own name and she heard that no one would be making a phone call. It was quiet after that. There was a glass of water on the table beside the bed and she reached for it and drank. Her lips were cracked and they hurt. There was a window behind her head that offered the evening light, and on the opposite wall hung a painting of Jesus feeding a large crowd.

After a bit there was a knock at the door and Isabella called out that it was dinnertime. Are you awake?

Yes, yes, she said, and she rose and looked at her baggy clothes and she straightened her hair in the mirror and saw that her face was puffy. She entered the kitchen and found Isabella and a man sitting at the table. There was a third place set and Isabella motioned to it and told her to sit. The man did not look at her. They ate chicken stewed with peppers and dried tomatoes, ladled over rice, and a green salad with avocados and tomatoes and cucumbers. She had never tasted anything so delicious and she said so.

Isabella said, I'm happy for you. The man grunted. He was a large man with lots of hair and his face had hair as well, and the one time she saw his eyes, she noticed that they were very blue. She looked, and looked away.

The man and his wife talked about water, and they talked about cattle, and they talked more about water and rain. As they had when she first woke, the woman spoke Spanish and the man English, and this was strange, because they believed that she only understood Spanish. And because it would be embarrassing to reveal the truth now, after all this time had passed, she let them believe what they believed.

When the man had finished eating he put down his utensils and looked at her and said, What do you think's going to happen here?

Isabella said, She doesn't understand.

The man repeated his question in Spanish.

Jack, stop it.

She looked at the man. She did not know the rules that this man carried in his heart and in his head. But mostly in his heart, because it was the heart that might alter the rules slightly, bend them, and it appeared that this man was not interested in the rules of the heart. Only the rules in his head. She was surprised to hear him speak Spanish so well, but then of course he had a Spanish wife.

How old are you? the man asked.

She looked at Isabella, who was looking at her. Seventeen, she said.

The man shook his head. You have family here? In America? When he said the word "America" he put a finger on the table as if to indicate a solid place.

She nodded.

Legal family? Your family. They are American citizens?

My boyfriend, she said. He's American.

And you walked here?

Here? she said.

To America.

She said that she had been in a van. And she had crossed two rivers.

Christ, the man said in English. And then he said, in Spanish, Yours is not a new story.

Enough, Isabella said. It's finished.

At night, she dreamed of the boy. And she dreamed of her mother and she dreamed of the baby. She woke and drank from her glass of water, and then she fell asleep again and this time she did not dream.

At breakfast, the man was not in the house. Isabella fed her pancakes with syrup and she managed to eat a little. She also drank a cold glass of milk, even though she wasn't fond of milk. After breakfast, Isabella told her to gather her things. She took her backpack and she took Gabriel's shoe. She climbed into the pickup beside Isabella. As they drove, Isabella advised her. She said that Íso should be careful of strangers. She said that if she had any money she should keep it hidden. Do you have money?

Íso nodded.

Enough?

Yes.

Is it safe?

Yes.

Do you have a destination? An address?

Yes.

You should know where you're going and what you're doing, Isabella said. Even when you're not sure, make it appear that you are sure. Don't cross the street against a red. Obey every rule. Don't draw attention to yourself. This won't be easy.

If you see the police, and you will see many, keep walking. Don't look. Don't look at any man. Even when someone shouts at you or wants to say something to you, especially on the street, just keep going. Don't let them know you're different. Learn English. Men will want to suggest things to you. You're good looking. You're young. Do you understand? Even so, a man can give you power, especially the one with money. But having money doesn't mean he's better, or kinder, or smarter. Never smarter. Just greedier. Be aware of the man with money. And the one without. She said that she had little respect for most men, and she had little respect for authority, and she had no respect for history, for it was a fact that men and authority and history were tied together like three pieces of rope. When you find a man, she said, and you will, he must be at your feet. My Jack might be a bit of a village brute but deep down he's soft. That's why when I get home today he might pretend to be angry, but he'll get over it. He's at my feet. This is how we live. Okay?

She nodded. She said, I'm sorry for the trouble.

Isabella didn't answer.

At the edge of the city, which was called San Antonio, they stopped at a Target and Isabella bought Íso jeans and two T-shirts and some underwear and a new bra, tennis shoes, and a pair of soft boots that Isabella called necessary in order to fit in. Íso put on her new boots and clothes in the change room and when she came out Isabella took the borrowed clothes and looked her up and down and said, Better.

She wanted to drive her to the central bus station, but Íso said no. It's enough, she said. And so Isabella drove her to a bus stop and gave her directions for downtown. She handed her a lunch of chicken quesadillas wrapped in plastic, and an orange, and two bottles of water. She told her not to get lost. She hugged her and said, Good luck, Íso. And then she drove away.


SHE took what she thought was the correct bus, but then she got off too soon, and she was lost. She sat on a bench at another bus stop and she watched the cars and the people, and each time a bus came by it stopped and the doors opened and people got off and people got on, but she just sat there. She saw that many of the people who rode the buses were poor and it reminded her of home, though these people here did not look at you, nor did anyone say hello. At some point she stood and began to walk. She had the new clothes she wore and she carried her small pack with its extra sweater and she still had the money that she had once again taped to her stomach. She also had Gabriel's shoe in her pack. And the lunch from Isabella.

She ate the lunch in a park where some boys were skateboarding. She watched them as she ate and when she was done she drank some water and she licked her fingers and spilled a bit of water onto her hands and cleaned them. She drank some more and then put the cap on the water bottle. The boys were filming each other, bending low to record their performances. They showed no interest in her. She imagined that it would be very easy not to be noticed. She sat for an hour in the sunshine. One of the boys passed by, near to her, and he looked at her and said hello in English and she was so surprised to be addressed that she said nothing.

The boy passed by again and stopped. Hey, he said.

She said hello and then she asked in English where the bus station was.

Downtown, he said. He pointed.

She looked in that direction.

'Bout ten minutes. And then he said, Peace, and he kept moving.

She stood and began to walk. The sun was hot and she was

thirsty and so she drank and she thought of water and heat and she pushed these thoughts away and kept walking. She thought about the boy's voice and how happily he had said the word "peace."

At the bus terminal she stood inside where it was cool and she watched the people. She found an empty spot on a bench and she sat and waited. The signs in the terminal were in Spanish and English and she heard many people speaking her language. An older woman passed by speaking in the accent of her place, where she had come from, and her heart lifted and she wanted to follow the woman, but she was gone. She sat for an hour, watching. She saw where people bought tickets and she saw them climb on the buses, but she was afraid to move forward, and she felt very tired. There were police with guns standing at all the entrances, but this did not surprise her, as she came from a place where a Coca-Cola truck had its own guard with a shotgun. Still, the police here seemed more frightening, and with their dark glasses it was difficult to know if they were looking at you or at something else. She fell asleep and woke when her head fell to her chest. She looked around but nobody was watching her, and so she closed her eyes and slept in little bits, waking to make sure she was safe, and then discovering that she was fine, and sleeping some more.

She woke and went to the bathroom and peed and then washed her hands and her face and dried herself with a paper towel.

She turned back into the terminal and saw that the line for the tickets was shorter, and so she walked over and stood behind a large man wearing a cowboy hat. He was eating a hot dog. She smelled it and felt her hunger.

When it was her turn, the ticket woman looked at her and waited. Íso said nothing.

Where ya goin'? the woman asked.

How much for one ticket to Saint Falls?

Return?

One way, she said.

Seventy-nine dollars, the woman said.

Íso bit her lip and looked around and then asked if the bus to Saint Falls went through Houston.

Houston's east. You wanna go north.

How much is a ticket for Houston?

Thirteen.

She thought about this but because the woman seemed impatient she said thank you and she stepped out of the line.

She didn't want to lift her shirt in public in order to get at her money, and so she went back to the bathroom and locked herself in a stall and lifted her shirt and tore away at the tape and plastic and slipped out five twenty-dollar bills. Then she sat on the toilet for a long time and she looked at the money, and she counted it, and she held it and counted it again. Finally, she took one of the twenties and put it in her pocket and she took the remaining eighty dollars and slid it back under the tape with her other money and she patted her shirt back down. The lineup was long again, and so she stood and waited and when it was her turn she bought a ticket to Houston.

The woman handed her the ticket and told her the gate number.

Íso said thank you. She sat on a bench close to the gate and she ate an apple and she chewed slowly and thought that she might come to regret her decision. Her heart, heavy with doubt and anguish, wanted to go straight north towards her baby, but she knew that there was a mother in Houston who needed to hear about her son. And there was only one person in the world who could give her that news.

SHE was seated alone and she curled up using the two seats and breathed air that was neither cool nor hot but stale, and she fell asleep at the end of the city and as the road fell out behind them and the coach rocked, she saw in her sleep the life she had left behind, and she saw the boy lift his face and ask her how soon, and she saw the damp rag on the boy's face and the sand drifting across the mound that was his body.

It was raining when she arrived but she didn't mind and she walked in the rain, stopping in bus shelters to take out the map that she had received from a man at the downtown bus station. The man had said about a three-hour walk, straight up Main Street. There were beggars, and that surprised her, but she ignored them, or she crossed the street. And when she saw a large group of boys walking towards her, she crossed back over to the other side of the street. There was the sound of sirens in the air, and there was smoke rising from a distant part of the city, and she saw men running and police cars riding by, sirens screaming. She stepped into the shadow of a building and watched the cars and the running crowds disappear. When it was quieter, she stepped back out into the street. She found crackers wrapped in little packages in a hamburger place, right next to Dollar & Deals. She filled her water bottle and took the crackers and she was eating them as she walked. She took small bites and the crackers melted in her mouth and then she drank a little water to wash everything down, and then took another small bite.

She arrived at what she thought might be the mother's place. The number was right, and the street was right, but she didn't trust herself and so she stood and watched the apartment block, which was five storeys high. There were broken windows and there was laundry hanging from balconies, and she saw a man and a woman arguing on one of the balconies. And then they went inside. It was no longer raining and there was a large area in front of the apartment block where children were playing. They spoke Spanish, all of them. She watched from a distance and then approached a young boy and asked if Señora Beatrice Aberquero lived there.

Yes. Number 333. He pointed, and ran off.

She entered the lobby and climbed the stairs and knocked on number 333. She held Gabriel's shoe. Her hands were shaking. The woman who answered was young. She wore a yellow skirt and a yellow shirt with her name, Beatrice, on it. She was barefoot. She looked at Íso and she looked at the shoe and she must have known because she made a sharp sound in her throat.

Íso looked down. My name's Íso Perdido, she said. It's your son.

The mother took the shoe. Gabriel, she said.

Yes, Íso said.

Where is he?

Íso shook her head. He's gone, she said.

The mother said the son's name again and she turned and went inside and the door was still open and Íso could hear her inside and it was as if she was talking to someone.

She waited. She could smell something cooking. She stepped inside and closed the door. The mother was sitting at the table, alone, the shoe before her. She looked up and motioned for Íso to sit down. Please.

She did.

You're hungry, the mother said. And thirsty.

Yes.

I have a lot. Please.

The mother stood and placed the shoe on her chair. She took a bowl from the cabinet and she ladled food into the bowl and she placed it before Íso. It was stew, or soup, and it smelled of meat and tomatoes and beans.

Please, the mother said, and placed a bottle of hot sauce and a tortilla before her.

She ate a full bowl while the mother stood and watched, and then she took another.

When she was finished eating, the mother picked up her bowl and cleaned it in the sink, and then she turned and asked about her son. Tell me, she said.

Íso lowered her head and told the mother about the boy. Then she said, I'm sorry, señora. And she began to cry. She put her face into her hands, and the noises she made surprised her, but she could not stop. The mother sat and touched Íso's knees with her own, but she herself did not cry. She waited until Íso had finished and then she said that there was nothing to be done, that Íso had done everything possible.

And then she whispered that Íso was welcome to stay for the night. Stay, she said. This is my home. You are welcome.

# 7.

She stayed a week with Beatrice, gathering strength, and during that time, when Beatrice was at work, she went out and investigated, and she discovered a nearby library where she could sit in a comfortable chair and watch the people come and go. There were many regulars who looked poor, and who seemed to think that the library was their living room. They played chess and they sat in groups and talked, and very few of them were interested in the books. Returning home in the afternoon, she usually stopped and bought groceries, and then made supper. Beatrice was very pleased, and so they sat in the evenings and shared the meals and talked. On her second-last day, she set about to make a special dinner for Beatrice. She fried chicken legs in oil and she baked beets in the oven and she opened a tin of corn and fried that in a pan with red peppers, sprinkling it with chilies. As they ate, Beatrice wanted to hear again about Gabriel, what he was like, and so Íso repeated what she had already said, that Gabriel was a beautiful boy who was full of curiosity and energy. He was very strong, Íso said. And she flexed her arms like a body builder. And then Beatrice said, But not strong enough. They were silent for a time, and then Beatrice spoke of Gabriel's birth, what a fighter he was, and of his father, who still did not know that his son was dead. I cannot, Beatrice said. Not yet. His father has nothing, and I have something, and so we thought that Gabriel's life would be better here, with me. And so he sent him. He shouldn't have.

That night Gabriel came to Íso in a dream and she asked him what it was like to be dead, and he said that he wasn't dead, he was only gone for a bit, and she woke from this dream and knew that she had to leave.

The following day, when Beatrice was at work, Íso went to the bus station where she'd first arrived, and she bought a ticket to Saint Falls for the next morning. The ticket was almost one hundred dollars one way, and after paying, she had seven hundred and forty-three dollars remaining in her pocket. That night she told Beatrice that she would be leaving.

Of course, Beatrice said. It is time.

I'm sorry, Íso said.

No, it's clear.

In the morning, Beatrice gave her a lunch and a dinner for the bus, and she passed her an envelope and said that it was necessary. You took care of my son, she said. She had not cried up to this point, and now there were tears in her eyes, but she brushed them away. She said that she would go home soon. To her husband. And they would have another child. We do foolish things sometimes, she said. I was foolish.

Then she touched Íso's face, and she touched her shoulder, and she hugged her.

Beatrice had made chicken sandwiches and boiled eggs and there were apples and bananas and carrots. Coconut cake and a chocolate bar. As the bus left the city limits Íso munched on the carrots and watched the landscape slide by and she thought that there was no more beautiful place than her home on the lake.

She had written her mother a message on one of the computers at the library, and she said that she was safe, and she was living with a woman in Houston for a time, a woman whose son had travelled with her, and that she would be travelling farther north very soon. She said that she would write only if she was having trouble. Having little contact is best. If you don't hear from me, that means I am safe. And then she wrote, Do not worry. It is all good.

THE city of Saint Falls and the land around the city was flat, and travelling in by bus she'd seen the Mississippi, and she'd seen large fields the colour of gold and in the fields were machines and trucks and there was a grey dust that rose into the air and obscured the sun. The days were long, and the nights were short, and even though she arrived at nine in the evening, the sun was just setting when she climbed from the bus. She spent the night at the bus station and tried to sleep but a security guard kept waking her. She was told that sleeping wasn't allowed in the station.

She left the station and wandered the streets. It was very quiet, and the part of the city she found herself in appeared to have no houses, and the stores and restaurants were all closed. She saw and heard a train at around 1 a.m., and after that there were no more trains. Cars were few. The first time she saw a police car she stepped into the entrance of a building and pressed herself against the wall. The police car passed slowly. She saw the heads of two men inside the car. They didn't look at her. She kept off the streets then. She found a sheltered place behind the stadium, inside an alcove that led to two large metal doors. It was dark in the alcove and private and she laid out a sweater on the concrete and used her backpack as a pillow and she slept and woke and then slept some more. When she woke in the morning she saw a pair of boots without laces and she saw bare legs and knees and she sat up quickly to discover an abuela standing over her, staring intently as if to figure out her reason for being. The abuela stood beside a shopping cart that was full of plastic bags that in turn were full of emptied and crushed cans. The abuela said, Ya can't be here. Her voice was quick and whispering and at first Íso didn't understand her, and then the abuela repeated the words and Íso gathered up her sweater and her backpack and began to move on.

The guards'll get ya, she said. Lock ya up.

When Íso looked back she saw the abuela moving away, pushing at her cart as if it were a large boulder.

In a fast food restaurant on one of the main streets she used the toilet and washed her hands and face. Other women came and went, and when she had a moment alone she brushed her teeth quickly and rinsed her mouth. She bought a coffee and an egg sandwich and ate it sitting at a booth near the back of the restaurant. There was very little Spanish spoken here. She'd noticed that already on the bus riding north. The closer they got to Saint Falls, the more English she heard. She wondered what colour of hair the baby had. At birth her hair had been dark and her eyes had been black, but Íso knew that colours could change as a baby grew, especially the eyes. She wondered what name the doctor had given the girl. Her mother had wanted her to name the girl, but Íso said that there was no point in naming a child she couldn't hold or speak to.

She finished her sandwich and held her coffee cup in both hands. It would be a warm day, it had already felt warm when she woke. She had an address, and she planned to find a map of the city, and she planned to locate the house where the doctor and his wife lived with her baby. Beyond that, she had no plans. She returned to the bathroom and used it once again, and then washed her face once more, and she looked at herself in the mirror and thought that she was okay. Her chapped lips had healed, and her eyes were no longer puffy, and she looked normal, though her T-shirt was a little dirty. She went back into the bathroom stall and changed into a clean shirt. She still had the money taped to her abdomen and she thought that now that she had arrived, she might be able to carry the money in her pocket, or her backpack.

Outside, standing on a street corner, a young woman holding a dog on a leash smiled at her, and Íso took this as a good sign, and she asked the young woman where she could find a map of the city. The young woman said she wasn't sure, but maybe one of the hotels had a map to offer and she nodded up the street. The woman walked off. She was wearing sunglasses and so it had been difficult to read what the nod had meant. Íso wandered off in the direction of the nod. She saw the abuela with the shopping cart coming towards her, and so she turned around and walked back and crossed the street at a light and took the opposite side.

There was no hotel. Not that she could find. She went into a drugstore and asked if they sold maps of the city, and the young girl said that she could buy a map at the bookstore in the mall. She turned away before Íso could ask where the mall was located. She stepped outside. She was surrounded by tall buildings, and she had no sense of where the sun was, and therefore she did not know where she was. Though, even with the sun, she wouldn't have known where she was.

She walked. The streets were fuller now with men in suits and carrying briefcases, and women pulling suitcases behind them. The women were dressed in skirts and dresses and they wore high heels. Everyone walked very quickly, with great purpose, and no one spoke or even said hello to the others on the street. She came to the train tracks and she sat on a bench and watched as the trains came and stopped and as people erupted from the doors. Two policemen walked by and when she saw them she opened her backpack and pretended to be looking for something. When they had passed, she stood and walked away from them, and crossed the tracks at the green light, and she came up against a large building that had glass windows and inside the windows there were mannequins wearing beautiful clothes and she thought that this must be the mall.

She spent that day and the next walking and exploring the city, which was divided into rich and poor. The rich lived in enclaves that were numbered as zones and the poor lived in abandoned warehouses, or in small rundown shacks that appeared to circle the city centre. The rich worked downtown in buildings of glass and steel and then made their way back to the safe zones, and sometimes returned to attend games at the stadium or to sit in the cafés on the street. There were police everywhere, and the ones to be feared most were those walking, or on horseback, or on bicycle, for they were close to the ground and they moved slowly, their black helmets swivelling, looking for anyone who might be threatening. This meant anyone walking aimlessly, or anyone with a certain slouch or attitude, or anyone who looked reduced. And so, when she walked she did so with her eyes forward, striding decisively, as if she had a destination, even though she didn't. She learned that it was safer to be on a bus, because this meant you were one notch above the poorest, who had only their feet to move through the city. She learned that the poor sometimes rose up in protest, and that this led to battles and rock throwing and the bite of tear gas. One day she saw what she thought was a parade—many people marching in one direction down a large street, calling out, singing—and then the police swooped in and began to round up the people and everyone ran, Íso included, even though she was just a spectator. She found herself surrounded by bodies, and she smelled smoke and she heard shouting, and she was carried along with the crowd like a cork bobbing in a river. She fought sideways, trying to free herself, calling out, Please, and Help, and No. A police horse floated by and a club came down and hit the man beside her. He fell. She looked down at him, and pushed on, eventually escaping the crowd by stepping into a shop that sold computers. The owner was standing behind the counter. He held a rifle, and he pointed it at her and told her to leave. Out, he said. She stepped back into the street and hugged the wall until the crowd had dissipated. A few stragglers ran by, young men wearing bandanas and calling out again and again a single word that she finally recognized as "Pigs." The slap of shoes against the pavement. And then quiet.

She began to avoid larger crowds, though sometimes it was impossible. She continued to take refuge in her alcove by the stadium and one evening there was a game taking place and there were thousands of people inside the stadium and their voices rose in unison and the noise moved the concrete beneath her, and the noise moved through her body, and at one point the roar was like a mammoth choir, beautiful to hear. She might have been lonely but she wasn't. She was full of anticipation and vigour and hope. She had her map, and she had marked the spot on the map where the doctor's house was, and the map was in her backpack, dry and safe, and she had learned the bus route that she would take to get to the doctor's house, and she knew that it would take anywhere from thirty minutes to an hour. She planned to go in the morning. She sat and listened to the crowd, and she watched people pass by her alcove, and because she was in the darkness, no one paid her any mind. She ate the remainder of a hot dog that she had bought that afternoon, at a stand near a park. The smell had driven her to spend too much money, and she had immediately felt guilty, and so she'd eaten only half and saved the rest for now, here, in her shelter. She ate slowly. The bun was soggy. She drank water. She laid out her sweater and settled in, comforted by the noise of the crowd that she could not see. She woke to thunder. And lightning. The wind was driving the rain into her alcove and when she woke her sweater was soaked, and so she was wet as well. She stood and twisted the water from her sweater, her back against the cold rain. She spent the remainder of the night squatted against the far corner of the alcove, where it was driest, her head between her knees. The rain fell sideways and reached for her, soaking her shoes. In the morning, when the rain had finally quit to a slow drizzle, she walked to her restaurant and in the bathroom she warmed her hands and face on the hair dryer, and then she went into the stall and changed into dry pants and a dry T-shirt and then used the blower to dry her wet clothes. She bought coffee and warmed her hands on the cup and stared out at the wet street and the folks pushing past under their umbrellas.

She took the number 15 bus and transferred to the number 32 and within an hour, when she disembarked, it had stopped raining. The trees were still dripping and the cars that passed at great speed threw up walls of water and she stuck to the inside of the sidewalk so as not to get wet.

Zone 7, where the doctor lived, was a walled district with one entrance, and at the entrance stood two guards who allowed people to come and go. She approached one of the guards at the gate. He was young, almost a boy, and he held a rifle and he wore high black boots and a black uniform. He asked for her permit. She said that she'd come to visit a friend. The guard said that a visitor permit was required. She asked how she might get a permit.

The guard studied her carefully and said that her friend should have provided one for her.

I can't go in? she said.

The guard shook his head and turned away to deal with someone else.

She walked then, alongside the wall, which was tall and imposing. There were shrubs planted at the top, very green and beautiful shrubs, and at the base of the shrubs there was razor wire. She returned to the entrance and stood on the far side of the road and watched cars come and go. Occasionally pedestrians approached the gate and were allowed entry. These pedestrians were usually women or girls, and they carried bags and they appeared to be familiar with the guards.

She caught the bus back downtown, tired out, a deep sadness in her chest.

The previous day she had discovered a street downtown that had been blocked off to traffic, and so in the evenings there were only people walking, and there were restaurants that spilled out onto the street, and it was boisterous and friendly, and even though she didn't talk to anyone she felt that she might be like everyone else. That evening she heard music and she came upon a man, his trumpet case at his feet, playing for the crowd. There was a small gathering before him, at a bit of a distance, and the gathering emptied and filled, and then emptied again, but always as it emptied, there were a few souls in the crowd who stepped forward and threw coins or bills into the case at the man's feet. The man, upon noting the donation, would turn to the giver and nod and keep playing. Íso found a bench nearby and she sat and listened to the music, and as she listened she began to cry. She didn't understand where the tears came from, though the lonely sound of the trumpet made her heart heavy. She didn't want anyone to notice that she was crying, so she bowed her head and wiped at her face. At some point she stopped crying, and she raised her head and she watched the man play. He was tall and thin and he wore shiny black shoes and tight black pants and a white T-shirt, and his long arms coming out of the short sleeves were fantastic, like the legs of a spider, and she was most mesmerized by his arms. Elbows out. Head dipping. One time, as he finished a song, he thanked the folks, and then he turned and he looked right at Íso and he nodded. Then he played another song. She thought she might have been mistaken, but he did the same thing with next song. Nodded at her. She got up and walked off.

She slept in her alcove that night and the following morning she ate her breakfast sandwich and she washed her face and brushed her teeth, and she took the number 15 and the number 32 to Zone 7, where the doctor lived, and she stood on the far side of the street and watched the vehicles come and go. Most of the cars had dark windows, and so she could not see the occupants.

She returned downtown in the afternoon, and later that evening she found herself sitting on the bench listening to the trumpet player.

The following day, on the number 32 bus, she recognized a girl she'd seen entering the gates to Zone 7. Her physical features were like those of someone from the south, and Íso decided to take a chance and she asked the girl in Spanish if she worked in Zone 7. The girl looked at her and then said, Yes.

Íso asked the girl if she'd worked there a long time, and the girl said for two months. For a family.

Children? Íso asked, and the girl said that there were three young children. The girl turned away then, as if wishing the conversation to be over, but Íso wasn't about to let her go, and she asked if there were other jobs working for families.

The girl shrugged. Always, she said. They're always looking. But they like you to speak English.

Íso said that she spoke English.

The girl looked at her quickly, unbelieving, and then looked away.

Where do I go? Íso asked. To apply for a job?

The girl said that there was no one place to go. It was illegal. You have to be recommended. It's all by recommendation.

The bus had arrived at the stop, and the girl rose and got off. She was carrying a shopping bag and it was heavy, and so she walked with a bit of a list, leaning to the right. Íso sat in her seat and watched as the girl spoke to the guard, and then passed through the gate and disappeared.

That night she found her bench and listened to the trumpet player. It grew darker. There was the smell of smoke in the air. Word was that there were riots and looting taking place in Zone 3, a few miles distant from the city centre. The trumpet player noticed Íso, and when he had finished a set, he put down his trumpet and walked over to her and said, Hello, stranger.

When she didn't reply he said, You lost, girl?

She shook her head.

I see you every night.

Íso stood to go.

Whoa, girl. I ain't chasing you. I like you sittin' here. You bring me luck, I'd say.

He held out his hand. Chaz, he said.

She looked at his hand, and then shook it.

You have a name? he asked.

I do, she said, and she told him.

She speaks. Good. You have any favourite songs, Íso? he asked.

She shrugged. She said, I just like sitting here.

Okay, he said. Okay. He studied her. Thank you, he said. And he went back to his trumpet and picked it up and he blew the saliva from it and then he began to play the song that had so moved her the first time she'd sat on the bench. She was surprised and she looked at him quickly and then looked away, for he was watching her. She sat down again. She kept her head lowered and she heard the trumpet, and sirens, and people talking on the patio, and then Chaz was standing before her again. She saw his black shoes, and she looked up.

Hey, he said. You haven't escaped.

Can I buy you a drink? he asked.

I don't drink, she said.

All right, good. How about a Coke, or coffee?

I smell, she said.

He laughed. First time I heard that. Then he said, I don't think so.

Oh, it's true, she said. I need a shower. Why she was being so honest with him, she wasn't sure.

There's a Y, he said.

Why?

YMCA. It's not expensive. And they have hot showers. I can show you, but first a drink.

She nodded. She felt some fear, but she hadn't spoken to anyone for a week save the girl on the bus. And here was Chaz, and he was talking to her and she was incredibly lonely and she knew that she wouldn't have to say much and so she said, Okay.

He told her to wait there and he walked off. He'd left his trumpet and case sitting beside her and she saw that now she was in charge of it and she thought that he wasn't stupid. When he returned ten minutes later, he was carrying a Coke for her and a can of beer for himself. He sat. Opened the Coke and handed it to her. Opened his beer and said, Cheers, and he drank. Ahh, he said, blowing makes me dry.

She sipped at her Coke. He took a pouch of tobacco from his pocket and he fished for his papers and he rolled a cigarette and lit it. She looked straight ahead.

He said that this was his favourite time of the evening. The light goes away, he said, and the crowds thin out and the air is still and the night stretches out before me. He laid his hand out flat to the ground and stretched out his thin arm and she saw the night as he must see it, predestined.

He finished his cigarette and then he finished his beer. He said, I work summers here and go south for the winter. Make more here, though. Folks are generous. Maybe they're buying a spot in heaven, who's to tell. If I were God, I'd save them a place.

They sat. Both of them quiet now. He rolled another cigarette and this time she watched his hands work. He offered her one and she shook her head.

He lit the cigarette and said that he'd show her the Y. It wasn't far. It was safer than sleeping on the street.

He had an old bicycle and he strapped his trumpet to the rear rack and then he straddled the frame and indicated the saddle behind him and he told her to sit. She climbed on, holding his shoulder, and she felt the bone of his clavicle. She found a precarious balance and attempted to ride along without touching him, but it proved dangerous and when he called out that she might want to hold on, she grasped his waist. Her legs hung down and her feet scraped the pavement, and so she lifted her legs slightly and in this manner they rode through the streets. She felt conspicuous.

At the Y he went in and then came out and he said that there was room at the inn. He handed her a piece of paper with his address on it. You'll need to have an address, he said. Just to say where you come from. And then he handed her thirty dollars and said that she'd brought him luck and now he was paying her back. She tried to return the money but he wouldn't take it.

He said, Adios, and then he was gone.

Only later, standing in the hot shower, did she realize that he had spoken her language.

She had a bed in a dorm room with five other girls, and even though she was exhausted she didn't sleep well. The sound of the other girls' breathing was very strange and new. She'd heard a few girls talking before they slept. They'd woken her with their noise when they'd come in, and they'd talked in an accent—German, she thought—and after they were quiet she couldn't get back to sleep. It didn't bother her. She liked the safety of the other girls, their bodies, their noises, the clothes on hangers or lying on the floor or at the foot of the beds, waiting to be inhabited again.

Early in the morning, with the first hint of light through the window, she got up and took her backpack and checked out and walked back downtown and caught her regular bus. She saw the same girl get on and she went over to her and sat down and said in English that she knew how to speak English and she needed a job and would the girl recommend her to someone who was looking for a worker.

The girl was quiet for a time, and Íso was quiet as well. She waited. And then the girl said that she would ask, but it wasn't guaranteed at all.

She spoke Spanish like Íso, with the same locutions and the same accent, and though they were both aware that they came from Guatemala, neither of them remarked on it, for it was as if to remark, or notice, would be to admit that they were outsiders, and in need, and the last thing either of them wanted was to appear vulnerable. And so they ignored what was obvious, and it was only later, when they became close, that they spoke of themselves and their pasts.

What's your name? the girl asked.

Íso told her and the girl said that her name was Vitoria. And then she asked if Íso had references.

You, Íso said. Just you.

Vitoria raised her eyebrows and said again that she would ask. It isn't easy, she said.

Thank you, Íso said, and she stood and went back to her own seat.

LATE afternoon she returned to Zone 7 and when Vitoria exited the gate and caught her bus downtown Íso followed her and when Vitoria climbed off the bus she did so as well and followed her from a distance. Vitoria walked with her heavy bag and she crossed the walkway above the interstate, and then descended a greenway and disappeared beneath a bridge. Íso waited and watched from above, and when Vitoria did not reappear, Íso crossed the greenway and entered the shadows of the bridge and came upon an encampment with makeshift tents and lean-tos made from multi-coloured tarpaulins and at the centre of this camp a fire burned. A young man squatted before the fire. He looked at Íso and then he looked away and tended to a frying pan in which there were four fillets of fish. He turned the fillets and called out. Two other young men emerged from the tents and then a young girl appeared, and finally Vitoria. When she saw Íso she did not seem surprised. She indicated for Íso to step forward and join them. And so she did.

She was handed a tin plate with half a piece of fish and there was dried-out bread and beans spooned from a large tin and she ate like the others, squatting around the fire. No one paid her much attention and it was as if she had landed in an alien place where no one cared if she was dark or white or clean or rich or poor and the only assumption made was that she was hungry, and so she was fed. The other girl, the one who was not Vitoria, was very young and she huddled beside the man who had made the food, and she didn't eat. She held the cook's arm and watched him eat and when he offered her a bite, she refused. Her hair was dirty and she was thin and she didn't speak. Later, she disappeared into one of the shelters with the cook and Íso never saw them again. Vitoria sat beside Íso and asked her if she had a place to sleep and Íso said that she was okay. Vitoria shrugged and said that there was always room here. You are welcome, she said. One of the other young men, who had a thick and black beard, said that he had room in his tent if she needed a place.

Vitoria told him to be quiet. He's always looking, Vitoria said to Íso.

Vitoria herself seemed to be attached to the third man. He would touch her head as he passed her by, as if indicating posses-sion, and when the food was finished Vitoria took his plate from him and he spoke to her softly in Spanish. Then, Vitoria sat beside her man and he smoked and held her hand. The traffic rumbled and clapped overhead, but this seemed of no concern. Time slowed down. Íso felt sleepy. She rose and gathered her bag and she said thank you and she walked out from under the bridge and up the greenway to the stairs of the bridge that would carry her over the interstate and down into the middle of the city. She had imagined that the others might call out or ask her to stay longer, or that Vitoria might speak, but none of this occurred.

SHE was persistent, and this being so she rode the bus again the following day, hoping to see Vitoria. When Vitoria climbed onto the bus she came right to her and sat down beside her. Vitoria's hands were very clean, and her hair smelled of fruit, and so she must have washed, and Íso wondered how she had managed that. Vitoria sat quietly for a bit, and then she said that if Íso wanted a job in Zone 7, she would need a health certificate. She said it was mostly for TB but there were other diseases the rich were worried about. Especially if you're coming from the outside. Which you are. She said she knew of a doctor who could do a physical. It would cost twenty dollars. Do you have that much? she asked.

Yes, Íso said.

I'll take you, then. On the weekend.

Thank you.

And then Vitoria said that the man wasn't her boyfriend. He just thinks he is. She spoke softly and apologetically, as if she might be confessing something. She said that it was safer to have a man than to be alone. To be alone was like an invitation, and wasn't it better to choose than to be chosen? She said that Íso should find someone, and if Íso needed help doing this, she would aid her. She said that the idea might go against her morals, but reality always smothered principles. A man is a man, she said. She said that Íso should stop riding the bus. It was too expensive.

Just before she got off, she said that there was a couple looking for a worker four days a week. They didn't have children, so it would be cleaning and shopping and dog walking. Very easy, but the pay wouldn't be great. She asked if Íso had permit papers.

Íso shook her head.

No one has papers, Vitoria said. But you'll need the medical certificate. And she said they should meet Saturday morning at the greenway.

THURSDAY evening, alone, she walked and walked. At one point, crowds of people were walking against her, moving towards the stadium. She put her head down and pushed forward into the commotion, banging shoulders with the passersby, hearing them speak, and their bodies and their voices were like scraps of wood that she received, and with these scraps she fashioned a raft upon which she floated, and she turned the raft and moved downstream with the crowd. She found her alcove, lay down on her sweater, felt the roar of the crowd, and heard the choir of seventy thousand voices.

The night was very warm and very humid and she left her alcove and pushed the sleeves of her T-shirt up onto her shoulders and she found her place on the bench and she listened to Chaz. He kept wiping the sweat from his forehead, and then he'd wipe his hands on his black pants. He nodded at her when she arrived and he looked at her between songs. The looks he gave her were easy.

That night, after his set, he asked her if she was still enjoying the Y and she said that she had moved out.

Too nice for you? he asked.

I have a place, she said.

With a shower?

She shook her head.

Are you safe in that place without a shower? he asked.

She said that she was safe. She could take care of herself.

Of course you can.

He rolled a cigarette and smoked. He asked if she was hungry.

She said that she was sometimes hungry.

Come, he said, and he pulled her to her feet. His hand was very large. She felt small.

He took her to a grocery store and they bought eggs and bread and cheese and peppers and onion greens and bananas and yogurt and jam. He said that he was going to make her breakfast at midnight.

She said that she couldn't go. She wasn't hungry anymore.

Ah, don't be frightened. Chaz isn't dangerous. He said that he lived with his sister and her child. Come, he said. You'll meet them.

And hearing that there was a sister, she was less fearful, and so she rode behind him through the streets into a dark area of town where there were no street lights and where young boys and girls ran in packs, and Chaz seemed to know all these children, for he called out to them, and they to him. He locked his bike and she followed him up a long metal staircase attached to the outside of a building and through a screen door into a room where a large woman sat holding a child. The woman said Chaz's name and then she said, Who's this? and Chaz said, This is my friend Íso. Íso, this is Rita and her baby, Sutt.

Sutt was bouncing on Rita's lap and sucking his fist.

Hi, Íso said, and she looked at the child and said his name, Sutt.

He don't speak yet, Rita said. Just eats and burps and shits. Gotta love him, though. She tweaked Sutt's cheek and he kicked his fat legs and looked up at his mother and gurgled. Sucked some more.

Chaz cooked while Íso sat on the couch and listened to Chaz and Rita talk. Chaz talked about this being the girl who'd brought him luck, and she was going to stay the night, in the guest room, after he'd fed her good.

Rita laughed and said that Chaz was always bringing home strays. You watch out for that boy, she said to Íso. And don't be thinking that when he says "guest room" you'll be at the Hotel Ritz.

Chaz said that he was the gentlest man in the neighbourhood. And anyhow look at her, he said, indicating Íso. Thin as a dime.

They ate scrambled eggs on toast and then toast with jam and then yogurt and toast and then some toast with coffee. Chaz stood

at the counter and sang as he produced the food and then Sutt
was in Íso's lap and she had her arms around him and she kissed
his curly hair as he chewed on her wrist. When they were done
eating, Rita gathered up Sutt and walked through a door from the
kitchen into another room. She shut the door behind her, and Íso
and Chaz were alone.

I have to go, Íso said.

Chaz took out his tobacco and asked if she would roll him
one while he cleaned up. He gave her the package and the papers
and then he stood and cleared the dishes. He ran water and soap
into the sink and set the dishes into the water, turned off the tap,
wiped the counter, dried his hands, and sat down across from Íso,
who was struggling with the cigarette. She held it up finally and
Chaz took it, studied it carefully, and then put it in his mouth and
lit it.

He exhaled and said, Made by Íso. He gestured down the hall.
There's an extra room. You'll sleep there. Even has a lock on the
inside in case you're worried about Sutt breaking in. He grinned.

He's handsome, Íso said.

He is that. You have children? he asked.

She said that she did, and then she said that she didn't.

Which is it? he asked.

No more, she said.

He nodded slowly and then ashed his cigarette and he said that
he was sorry.

He finished his cigarette and he said that he was going to sit
up for a while and listen to music, and she could do as she pleased.

He pointed to where the bathroom was and he said that she might want to shower. It's all yours. Though there's no hot water. Can't have everything when you squat.

She didn't know the word "squat," and she didn't ask.

He stood at the sink while she crept down to the bathroom and locked the door and sat on the toilet. She could hear him humming some song. He had a clear voice. She didn't want to shower. It felt too strange. And so she found the bedroom he'd indicated and she locked herself in, and she lay on the bed fully clothed and she immediately slept. She dreamed of the doctor, who was now fluent in Spanish, and it pleased her that the doctor had dedicated himself to learning her language. And then the doctor was holding her baby and he set the baby on the floor and the baby toddled over to her and she scooped it up and up and up and then they were flying. She woke from this dream and she knew that her baby was too young to be walking. She had a sudden thought that her child might be dead, but she put that thought aside and imagined her girl sleeping out there in the city somewhere, and her shoulders ached and she realized that she was holding her breath and that her heart was beating wildly. It took her a long time to fall asleep again.

She woke early and tiptoed to the bathroom and stripped and showered quickly, shivering under the cold water, worried that she might be caught. Most of her clothes were dirty, but she found the cleanest possible, dressed, and then slipped out of the bathroom and through the kitchen and down the staircase to the street below. She walked down to the river and watched the water tumble through the spillway.

She found her way back downtown and in a park near the stadium she sat on the grass and watched a troupe of young girls, ballerinas, perform on a small stage. There was a smattering of a crowd—mostly parents, it appeared—and when the dance was finished, the small crowd offered applause and Íso joined in.

Mid-afternoon, she returned to Chaz's place and found him eating at the kitchen table. Sutt was in a high chair beside him.

Look at you, Chaz said when she entered.

Can I come in? she asked.

Mi casa and all that, Chaz said. Hungry? He pointed at the cooker.

She took a bowl and ladled some soup into it and she sat and began to eat. Chaz was feeding Sutt soup as well, just the broth and a few mashed-up carrots.

She ate. And then took another bowl.

Chaz said that Rita was out scavenging, looking for food and such, and he had to go out for a bit and would she mind looking after Sutt. Just for an hour. He likes the outdoors, so if you want to walk him in the stroller, you can.

She was surprised. She couldn't imagine taking care of a child. She'd already lost two children, her own and then Gabriel, but of course Chaz couldn't know that. No one could know that. And so she nodded and said that she would be happy to take care of Sutt.

His diaper's clean. He's fed. He'll probably just sleep.

When she was alone with Sutt she laid him on her bed and watched him roll from side to side. He touched her face, and then studied her hand. He hiccupped. He yawned. His cheeks were fat and his hands were fat and his skin was perfect like his mother's, and like Chaz's. All three were the same colour, brown going on black. He closed his eyes, opened them, and then closed them and he slept. She kneeled beside the bed and did not move for an hour. She stroked his face and his arms and she talked to him. She said that he was beautiful and that he was strong and that he was lucky. She said that she loved him, and saying this she realized it was true, that love for a child, even a strange child, might fall down immediately on the head of the keeper. Sutt shuddered as if a dream were rising up through his eyelids. He whimpered.

Oh, you, she said.

She heard Chaz return, and still she stayed where she was, as if afraid that if she let the baby out of her sight, he would disappear.

Chaz knocked and stood in the doorway and said, Aren't you two a picture.

He's beautiful, she said.

How old was he? Chaz asked. Your child.

One day, she said. It was a girl.

Jesus, Chaz said.

He was standing behind her now. She was kneeling and holding the baby's fingers, and he was standing behind her. She could feel him there.

Do not touch me, she thought. Do not.

You all right? he said.

She nodded.

Okay, he said, and she felt him move away.

When she came out into the kitchen holding Sutt, Chaz was

on the fire escape. He called out to her and she stood in the doorway holding the groggy baby and he pointed out over the city, to the north, and he said that the riots might spill over into other zones and that would bring down a curfew, as it usually did. That'll fuck things up good, he said. No more music for a while. Give, he said, and he held out his arms for Sutt. She handed him over.

SATURDAY morning she found Vitoria sitting on the greenway, a single bag at her feet. She rose and came towards Íso and took her hand and together they crossed via the pedestrian bridge. Down past the truck docks and the warehouses and over the railroad tracks into a small enclave of office buildings, where they stopped before a glass door and Vitoria pushed a button. The round eye of an all-knowing camera hovered above the doorway.

The doctor was young with dreadlocks and when he bent to place the stethoscope against Íso's chest she smelled the sweat in his hair. The posters on his walls offered diagrams of internal organs and the bones of the human body and there was a ceramic knee on his desk with exposed ligaments. He weighed her and took her blood pressure and he felt under her arms and asked her to open her mouth. He lit a flashlight and inspected her ears. He pressed a small vial against her upper right arm and said that this was a Mantoux test, for TB. She was to return in forty-eight hours, he would inspect it, and if she was clean she would get her certificate. His voice was soft and he spoke with the same lilting affect that she had come to know from Doctor Mann. When he slipped on gloves and advised her that he was going to do an internal she closed her eyes and turned her head away. When he was done, he sat and wrote on a piece of paper while she stood behind the partition and changed. He spoke. He asked her how old her child was. She paused while buttoning her shirt and then she said that her child was five months old. When she came out from behind the partition he handed the signed papers to her and he said that she was very healthy, though she needed to put on some weight.

She said that she would try.

Eat starch, and drink milk. More fat.

I'll try.

He asked if she had other family.

Yes.

Here?

Yes.

Good. Then he wished her all the luck in the world, and these words were strange coming from the mouth of a doctor.

Thank you, she said. She said that she would come back in two days.

Vitoria was waiting in the anteroom. Íso paid and then they walked out into the street together and she thought that now Vitoria would leave her, but they walked together in the sunshine, down into the streets of the city centre, and they bought and shared a hot dog and drank a bottle of water on the grass next to the stadium parking lot beneath a billboard that advertised a local fertility clinic. The image on the billboard was of a young woman holding a baby. The billboard was old and weathered and the young woman was missing an eye. The baby was naked and still had all its parts.

Vitoria asked her if she believed that things happened for a reason.

What things?

Good things. Evil things.

Man-made things?

Or those things brought on by God. Like earthquakes and tornadoes and floods. She said that she had witnessed a tornado in Kansas when she'd first arrived in this country. The tornado was dark and powerful and it had a sound like nothing she'd ever heard before. And so she could not compare it to anything else. It hurt her ears. The wind ripped up the earth and the trees and the houses and it tossed over vehicles like toys. It was more frightening than an earthquake.

You've been in an earthquake?

Yes, twice. But they were short, and not powerful. If they aren't powerful they are interesting. The ground moves, the lamps sway, the pictures on the wall shift. A tornado arrives like a lion.

You know a lion?

No. But I've seen movies, and heard the noises they make. She said that those were events directed by God. And then there were those events directed by men. She said that the night previous, their encampment had been raided. Soldiers had come and torn down the tents and destroyed their belongings. Everyone had been arrested.

But you?

I was fetching water. And when I returned I saw the lights and the cars and the horses with men in helmets and I saw the clubs and all I heard were the noises from the cars overhead on the freeway. I ran. And later I went back and found a few of my things. There was hardly anything left.

Íso was quiet. She said that she was sorry. You must be sad.

Vitoria shrugged. I was lucky, she said.

And the others? Your friends?

She shrugged again.

What will you do?

Find some new place. There are other places to sleep.

There's the Y, Íso said.

Too much money.

And so Íso did what she knew she must, though she also understood that her decision was a selfish one. She needed Vitoria.

Chaz was at the kitchen table, drinking coffee and smoking his morning cigarette, when they arrived. Sutt on his lap. He saw Vitoria and he looked at Íso and before she could speak he said that if the new girl was going to stay, she'd have to sleep in Íso's room. And then he grinned and said, Unless she needs someone stronger.

They ate that night, the five of them, by the light of a candelabra that Rita had found while out foraging. Falsely gold-leafed, it sat in the centre of the table while five candles of various sizes and colours guttered and waved. They ate fried sausages and peppers and old feta and they ate doughnuts for dessert. They drank coffee and water and Vitoria and Chaz shared a beer. Chaz liked it that

Vitoria was an imbiber, as he called it, and he asked where she had learned to drink.

Is it necessary to learn? she asked.

Íso here doesn't touch the stuff.

Is it okay? Íso? She was quite serious and would have handed back her beer if Íso had been offended.

Don't listen to him, Íso said. He likes attention.

And she saw that Vitoria was willing to give it. She was intrigued by Vitoria's comfort with Chaz, how effortlessly she spoke to him, how open she was. That night she lay beside Vitoria on their narrow bed and she asked if she had always found it easy talking to men.

Am I easy? Vitoria asked.

Not easy. But you're not afraid to speak, or to laugh, or to offend.

They were whispering, speaking their language. Íso was happy to have Vitoria's body beside her.

I learned young, Vitoria said. I was fourteen when my mother sold me to Daunte, the boss of the barrio where we lived. And she told Íso the story of her earlier life in the barrio flanking the garbage dump in Guatemala City. She said that her mother was a crier for garbage who had moved up to being a collector, and it was Vitoria's job to help her mother. They lived in a shanty that belonged to Daunte. Daunte was not a man in the real sense. He'd been castrated by his enemies at the age of twenty, but this had in fact obliged him to appear unscathed, and so he chose young girls from the barrio to visit him, to prove that he had a potent beak, and Vitoria had been one of those chosen.

He paid my mother, she said. A good amount. I didn't have to do anything except arrive at his house when he asked for me, dress up for him, watch soccer, eat pizza, kiss him on the mouth and stroke his feet. He liked to lie on the bed in his Adidas shorts and he'd speak to me as I rubbed his body with ointments and lotions. I returned to my mother in the morning. He had a guard named Julio who was much more dangerous, and it was Julio who sometimes visited my shanty and tried to get in and I always shouted at him that Daunte would kill us both, which was true, and so he sat outside my door and he wept. He was sentimental. Men can be very stupid. This is why it is easy to talk to them. They listen. Especially if you are young and if you praise them and call them handsome and kind and generous, which they might not be, but who will not believe lies dressed up as flattery?

She said that when she turned eighteen, Daunte found a younger girl, perhaps even two or three more, and so she was no longer wanted. Her mother had died two years earlier, and she was alone, and so she took the money she had saved, and she left and rode La Bestia up through Mexico and crossed the Rio Grande into America. I had a friend here, in this city, and so I came. Otherwise I would have gone to Los Angeles or San Francisco. My friend left last month.

Vitoria sighed. Yawned. Her story was just a story to her. The tale of her life. No better or worse than anyone else's tale. This was her nature. She asked about Íso, what was her story?

It's nothing, Íso said.

I'm sure it's something, Vitoria said, and she fell asleep.

Íso lay awake for a long time. Vitoria's story had given her courage. She felt strong. She thought that tomorrow she would begin to eat more. She would gain weight. She would store up fat for the time when she needed it.

THE couple was young. The woman was taller than her husband, even in bare feet, but she liked to wear high-heeled boots or shoes, as if it gave her great pleasure to look down on her husband. Íso always knew when the woman was home because she heard her heels on the floor and she smelled her, a citrus scent that she wore. The woman's name was Barbara, the man was called Chris. He worked in information and she was in finance. They had a driver who took them downtown every day and returned them to their house in the evening. Íso's job was to clean the bathrooms, of which there were four, and to vacuum, and to polish the kitchen from top to bottom, and to walk the dog, and to iron and fold laundry. Dry cleaning was taken care of by the driver, whose name was Oliver, and who sometimes drove Íso back downtown in the evening, if the husband and wife were late coming home and the buses had stopped running.

When they had interviewed her, she sat on a chair in their front room, and they sat on a white leather couch. Barbara had a notebook, and she kept referring to it, as if the notebook might tell her something important about Íso. Chris was more relaxed, he liked to joke, and he seemed impatient to get the interview over with. Barbara asked her if she had ever worked with foreigners before. She told them that she had. In her village, where tourists came because of the beauty of the lake. She described the lake and she told them about the volcanoes and she said that one could ride on horseback to the cloud forest and from there look down on the lake. It was popular. She said that she was an intern, and that she had worked at the hospital in the town, and that she had worked with doctors from America who had come there to volunteer. She did not make mention of the clinic. She understood that Barbara and Chris might speak to their neighbours, who in turn might speak to theirs, and in that manner the doctor and his wife might hear that there was a Guatemalan girl in Zone 7 who had worked at a fertility clinic. This was her reasoning.

Her English was good, of course, and this surprised Barbara, and it made Chris flirtatious.

He asked if she had a boyfriend.

She said that she didn't.

Barbara looked at Chris but she didn't say anything. She just looked.

Chris said that he'd love to visit the lake where she lived.

Do you have papers? Barbara asked.

She handed them her health certificate, which she had picked up the day before. She was clean.

Permit papers? Barbara asked.

Íso shook her head. No.

We might be able to arrange something, Barbara said. In any case, it's impossible to find workers. Everyone is struggling.

Íso agreed that everyone was struggling.

If you're asked by the authorities where you work, Barbara said, you can't say.

Of course.

This job isn't a job.

Yes.

It doesn't exist.

Yes.

Chris laughed. What can happen? he said. They arrest us.

No, Barbara said. They arrest Íso. And we lose her. And she is deported. She turned back to Íso and said that she would be given a test run. For a week. And then they would re-evaluate. She would have a key to the house. And the security code. She would have a pass to enter Zone 7. She was not to give that pass to anyone else. Barbara told her how much she would be paid, and when. Íso did not let on that this was a large amount, much more than she'd earned at the clinic.

She worked in the afternoons, starting at one. After the first week, Barbara told her that she was good. She could stay on. The house was silent, and if she had been inclined towards loneliness, she would have felt terribly isolated. As it was, she was happy to be alone. The house had security cameras, inside and out. Of course, there were cameras everywhere in the city as well—on the buses, on street corners, in restaurants and malls—but she was surprised to see cameras in the house, where Chris and Barbara lived private lives. Only the bathrooms were free from cameras. She liked to spend time in Barbara's bathroom. It reminded her of the tiled and scented massage rooms at the clinic. The low hum, the cleanliness, the soft white towels, the privacy. She went through Barbara's toiletries. Makeup, lipstick, eyeliner, pills, vitamins, face wash, tweezers, four different sizes of nail clippers, condoms, bars of soap, facial scrub pads, deodorant, perfume, shaver, cream, hand lotion. She sometimes took a little lotion for her hands when she'd finished cleaning. It was rich and creamy and thick. It had no scent.

She didn't have to cook. Chris did that. Though she was required to help at dinner parties, alongside the caterers. During these dinner parties she usually stayed in the kitchen and helped the chef, or she cleaned up the bathrooms if someone had left a mess, which seemed to happen quite often. One time she came upon a couple in the shower. She heard voices, caught a glimpse of the couple, stepped back, and went downstairs to the kitchen. This was the same dinner party where Barbara had hired five young women to walk around topless and serve hors d'oeuvres and canapés. Íso was in the kitchen, and when the girls returned to fill up the platters, they talked amongst themselves, and a few of them, later in the evening, stepped out into the garden to have a cigarette. Smoking bare-breasted. Íso did not know where to look when the girls spoke to her, asking for something, and so she looked at their feet, but the girls didn't seem to notice Íso, and so she stopped looking at them altogether. She simply responded to their requests by pointing or gesturing. The one time she'd gone out into the main room, to help with the lighting of candles, the guests had appeared not to notice the young women.

Oliver drove her back to the city in the limousine late that night. He rarely spoke, though the one time she heard him talking to Barbara she knew instantly which country he came from. She was hungry and tired and her hands were shaking and she wanted to talk to someone, even if there was no response, and so she said to Oliver that the girls were very pretty.

He grunted.

You're from Russia, she said.

If he was surprised he didn't show it. He shrugged and asked how she knew.

I recognize the voice.

The accent, he said.

Yes. The accent.

He said that a girl was pretty for only a moment. He said that being beautiful was like a fog—it made everyone blind. You understand? The boy, the girl, the other boy, the other girl. And then you grow up and the fog is gone and you find out the truth.

Íso was surprised by this long speech. She said that the girls were smoking in the garden. Without their shirts.

Oliver grunted, and then he said, You'll get used to it.

Do you have family? she asked. This was forward of her.

He was quiet. Then he said he had a little boy who was still in Russia. And you? he asked.

No. Nothing, she said.


ONE night, late, there was a large fire downtown. Someone said it was a mall that had been broken into and looted, and she watched the fire from the balcony, along with Chaz and Rita and Sutt and

Vitoria. Neighbours gathered in the street below, and folks settled on chairs to watch the smoke pluming. It was like a carnival. Chaz said that the smell of tear gas meant there was a revolution happening. He grinned. The following day police on horseback rolled through the neighbourhood, gathering up vagrants. They clubbed those they caught, and chased down the runners, and threw the captured into black vans. There were shouts and sighs and cries for mercy, but none of those watching, of which Íso was one, intervened. People were just happy to be above the fray.

She learned that those who had nothing to lose are the most dangerous. She learned that the young children who ran in packs didn't have fathers, and sometimes they didn't have mothers, and she thought that even where she came from, a family might be poor, but it was still a family. She learned that Sutt's father was in prison. She learned that Rita was adept at finding food in the dumpsters behind the supermarkets, and when she heard this she thought of her mother, who had arrived in this country years earlier and foraged for food in this manner. She learned that the "best before" date meant little, except for milk and cream. Yogurt and cheese could be eaten weeks after that date—you simply had to remove the mould. And so she learned to eat yogurt and cheese, even though these things made her mouth curl. She learned that Vitoria was fond of Chaz and vice versa. Sometimes at night Vitoria was absent and Íso knew that she had gone to visit Chaz in his room. This did not bother her, though she missed the comfort of Vitoria's body and she missed her voice. She had not yet told Vitoria about her baby, and she realized that she wouldn't tell her.

It was too dangerous. She learned not to think too much about what might happen, and she learned not to dwell too much on the existence of her child out there. She learned that her employers, Barbara and Chris, were fearful, not so much of the day to day, but of the possibility that what they had might be taken from them—their advantage, their safety—and this being so, they celebrated their fragile security by living extravagantly, by throwing large parties, and by spending large amounts of money on objects they would never use. She learned to be silent, and never to ask questions, and to do whatever was bidden. This was not difficult. She had learned the art of igual long ago, at the clinic, with the women who had come to take the waters at Ixchel.

For the most part, she was alone in the house four afternoons a week. She did her chores and then walked the dog, Champ, a dachshund. She carried plastic bags to clean up the dog's shit. She didn't like dogs, and she didn't like picking up shit. Barbara adored Champ, though Barbara rarely took Champ for walks, and if she did, she wouldn't pick up his shit.

She of course had a reason for being there, and so she became familiar with the neighbourhood. Because the streets were oddly placed, with many dead ends, it took her some time, but while out walking one afternoon, she found the doctor's house set back in a bay. A single manor sitting by itself, surrounded by fields of grass and flowers, with a view of a small river out back. She had the house number, and she had the correct street, but now that she had arrived, and was standing across from his house, she wasn't clear what her next step should be. There was no movement outside the house. In fact, no house in Zone 7 showed life. She walked back and forth along the far side of the street so as not to draw attention to herself, but as she was the only sign of life thereabouts, it was a fact that she would have been paid all the attention. If there'd been someone to pay attention.

Champ peed on the boulevard. Tugged at the leash. She backed away and then walked on. She returned the following day to find that nothing had changed. She was breathless, and she was dizzy with dread.

The river that wound through Zone 7 arrived via a tunnel that ran beneath the guard wall and passed behind the doctor's house and then moved south and eventually through another tunnel and back out into the unprotected world. There were paths on either side of the river, and footbridges, and there were benches placed in copses of trees for people to take advantage of the bucolic scene. There were public washrooms as well, situated at the beginning and the end of the path. This is where Iso took to walking Champ. It was quiet and away from the streets, and the path passed behind the doctor's house and she could pause and survey it.

It was on this path, late one afternoon, that she ran into the doctor. He was walking alone, and he was pushing a stroller. She saw him from a distance and she knew immediately. He was walking with long strides, as he had always done when they walked through the pueblos that surrounded the lake. Back then she had to skip or run to catch up to him, or she had to tell him to slow down. Now, as he approached her, he had both hands on the stroller and he was talking to himself, or perhaps he was talking to the baby. His hair was cut short, and he wore a paisley shirt and a purple scarf. He was so involved in talking that he did not see her, though she was standing on the path. The river was gurgling past. Or perhaps it was the child making noises in the stroller. She was aware of the stroller and of the noises. At first, when she recognized Eric and realized that her baby was with him, her legs had gone weak from surprise and fear and dismay. She had even considered turning away and walking in the opposite direction. But she didn't turn away. She stood in the path and as he drew near she grew calm and she said hello. He looked up. And then he said hello and in that moment she remembered everything about him.

THEY met on Monday and Wednesday afternoons, when he walked Meja for an hour. By the river path that led past the water wheel and down towards the elms that offered shade and privacy. On a bench near the footbridge beyond the public washroom. She was always there first, waiting, her dog at her feet. She heard them before she saw them—the sound of the stroller wheels on the packed gravel, his footsteps—and her heart leaped and she sat up straight and when they came around the bend in the path, she was always surprised, and grateful.

Sometimes he brought her a little treat, a piece of chocolate, or a candy, and she always said thank you and put the treat in her pocket. There was something childlike about this, the giving of candy. He was not the same man, he did not have the same confidence. And once, when he asked if he could kiss her, she said, Not here, not now, and she realized that the Eric Mann she had known at the lake would never have asked that question. He would simply have kissed her.

He had no curiosity about her. Did not even ask for her name. He just accepted her as a girl on a bench. Someone to talk to. He gave her the bare facts of his life. His name, his wife's name, the baby's name. He was very willing to answer all her questions, though he said that some questions might be more difficult than others. He had suffered a brain injury and his memory was confused. Though he remembered this, didn't he? He shrugged. She said that she was sorry for him. She asked him about Susan, and about the baby, Meja. She asked who had named the baby. Susan had. She asked if Susan breastfed. Oh no, she didn't. She asked if the baby was happy. Very. She asked if he was happy. He said yes, and then he said that he wasn't sure what happy meant, or what it felt like. This was the strange thing about his head. He couldn't even recall where Meja had come from. He said that Susan had brought her. Or that the baby had come to them.

Come to them!

The first time she met him, when he was talking to himself as he walked along the path, she had said hello, surprising herself with how calm she was, and he had looked up and then said hello, and in the manner he said hello she realized that he did not remember her. She said that it was a beautiful day and he agreed. She pointed to her dog and said, This is Champ. Hi, Champ, he said. He gestured at the stroller and said, This is Meja. Your baby? she asked. Yes, he said. And he bent to lift back the blanket. She bent with him and saw her child and she stopped breathing. She was whole, and alive. Her hands were bare and they were clenched in fists. Very small fists. Her knuckles. Her eyebrows. He covered the baby up and stood. She stood as well. She asked him if he lived nearby, and he said yes and pointed back over his shoulder towards his house. His voice was his voice. No different. His eyes, though, were different. Less clear, and his face was blanker. She said that she was going to sit on the bench. Do you want to? He did. He sat and clucked at the stroller. He smiled. He was still very handsome, even with short hair. His forearms were still strong. His fingers the same. She thought that she should hate him, but she didn't. He was ignorant. But perhaps he had always been ignorant. And selfish. And unaware. She had loved him so dearly that she might have missed some bigger flaw in him.

She had many questions that she could not ask, simply because they were too dangerous, and also because he wouldn't know the answers. She asked him his wife's name. Susan, he said. She's at work. He smiled blandly at his own statement. He did not ask her name, not then, or after. It was as if she was an object that had been placed on the bench beside him. She was angry, and then sad. She asked if she could look at the baby again. Of course, he said. She peeked into the stroller and saw her baby and she wanted to scoop up the child and run and run but she didn't. Her heart was full. The baby's eyes were black, and her lashes were long and black. Her cheeks were fat. She was well fed and healthy. Íso touched the baby's face and spoke Spanish and then realized that this revealed too much about her, and so she changed to English. She asked if she could hold the baby. Yes, he said, and he went to lift Meja from the stroller, but she said that she could do it. She bent forward and picked up the baby. She sat beside him on the bench and she looked down at her child and she said her name, Meja. She said it again. Meja wore orange socks that were rolled down and Íso touched the chubby flesh above the socks and she smelled Meja's head and she touched her ears and she passed a hand over her crown. The girl's hair was black and there was a lot of it and she felt its soft silk and realized that she might swoon. She swallowed and said that the baby was so strong. Meja had taken her hand and was gumming one of Íso's fingers. At some point Meja leaned back and studied Íso. Stared at her as if gauging how safe she was, but of course that was impossible. She's very smart, Íso said, and she drew Meja towards her chest and Meja clutched at her. A little monkey. The softness of Meja's wrists against her own neck. Meja made noises, as if she were a small truck starting up. Listen to you, Íso said. Listen to you.

It was on the second or third visit when she realized that the danger was not Eric but Susan. She looked at him and asked if this could be a secret, their visits. He was happy to agree. He said that Susan was a stickler for routines, and she disliked surprises, and she didn't know that he took these walks with the baby, and she would be upset if she knew that he was meeting a stranger by the river.

Okay, she said. This is our secret.

The visits were brief and the time between visits unbearable, and when they did finally meet, she wanted him to be quiet so that she could concentrate on the baby, but he saw her as a vessel into which he could pour information. Perhaps he was lonely. Perhaps no one ever listened to him.

He was very simple and concrete when he spoke. On Tuesdays and Thursdays he worked in his shop tearing apart and repairing small gas engines. His doctor had suggested this. There were days when he managed to put an engine back together, and there were other days when he had extra parts that lay loosely on his worktable. On Wednesdays he washed clothes and he ironed. On Fridays his nurse arrived and they worked on memory exercises and then his hairdresser came and she washed and shampooed his hair and sometimes cut it. He also received a manicure and a pedicure. When he told Íso this he held out his hands and she saw the perfection of his cuticles and his soft hands that she used to adore. She thought now that his hands were too soft and too white and too perfect. She was repulsed. He told her that he was often alone, and that their girl, Laura, was in charge of Meja, though Laura allowed him to walk Meja for an hour. Susan worked every day downtown. She left early and then returned in the evening and came looking for Meja and took her away to a room upstairs. They sometimes ate supper together, but usually Susan wanted to be with Meja until she was down for the night, and even after, in the dark of the evening, Susan was elsewhere. She was tired from work. She loved Meja and wanted to spend time with Meja. Susan and Meja slept together.

When she heard this, Íso was devastated, and she thought that she could not bear it, but she did. She took Eric's hand and held it. She asked if he had hope for his life, and he said that he didn't know exactly what hope was. She explained it to him. She said that hope was a wish, and of course hope couldn't exist without the possibility that what you wished for might not come to be. He thought about this and nodded. He said that every day when he walked the path with Meja, he hoped to see her.

Me too, she said.

One thing was certain: even though he did not remember her, he still loved her in his limited way. One afternoon he asked if he could give her a hug, and she allowed this. He held her and held her until she had to break free. He wanted to kiss her. She said that there might be a time for that, but not now. She discovered that she felt nothing for him except pity. He was vacant and her heart no longer had room for him. She allowed him to hug her because she knew that this was the path she must take. He was like a child rooting at her. One time, after holding her, he touched the necklace at her throat and his face went soft and he said, This. He was looking into the past, briefly recognizing something. She held her breath. Here was danger. And then he shook his head and released the necklace.

She left feeling dirty, and on the bus ride home she knew that what her uncle told her had come true: she had been attracted to an object that was beautiful, and she had become spellbound, and then its shape had changed, and what had appeared to be beautiful had turned ugly.

ON Thursday she worked late, and as she left to catch her bus, she went away from the exit and walked down towards the river and the doctor's house. It was close to 7 p.m. The sun fell onto the back of her head and left her with a sense of longing. She came to the bay where the doctor lived and she turned right, towards his house. She stepped off the sidewalk and stood behind a large tree and watched the house. She had no intent, just a desire to be close. She was about to leave when a car turned into the bay and pulled into the doctor's driveway. The driver's door opened and a woman appeared. The woman's hair was blonde, but it was cut very short, and for a moment Íso didn't recognize her. She wore a narrow white skirt and red high-heeled shoes and a grey flowing shirt and sunglasses. And then the woman swivelled her head just so, and she lifted a hand to touch her jaw, and in that movement of the woman's hand, so refined and tentative and self-conscious, Íso knew that this was the doctor's wife. Íso closed her eyes. Opened them. The doctor's wife was still there. Íso leaned against the tree to save herself from falling. Her chest ached and she felt the ache and she knew for the first time what pure hatred was. It was entire and it moved sideways and forwards and backwards within her, and it was as if she contained the deep waters of an ocean that had been shaken by an earthquake and what resulted were mammoth waves, waves that could not be held back. The doctor's wife bent into the back seat and reappeared, holding Meja. She was talking, moving her head close to Meja and then pulling back again. She did not remove her sunglasses as she spoke to the baby. Íso thought she heard Meja gurgle, though it was impossible at that distance, but still she was filled with despair. Of course Meja would adore Susan. And of course they were attached. And of course they had eyes only for each other. And of course Meja did not know Íso. And of course Íso did not know Meja. She tumbled into hopelessness, and then felt anger, and once again hatred, and of these three emotions, hatred gave her the most pleasure. She turned away and pressed her face against the bark of the tree. When she looked up again, Susan and Meja had disappeared.

Íso sat at the base of the tree until the light faded, and the pale sky turned grey and then ochre and finally black. The birds stopped singing in the branches above. All was quiet. She inspected her heart. The hatred had been exhilarating. And welcome. And crippling. And exhausting. And very dangerous. For passion, anguish, jealousy, and anger would produce nothing but mistakes, and false steps, and failure.

A cold heart was necessary.


THE weekend came and lasted forever. She washed her clothes and sewed patches on her jeans. At night she was alone, and she heard Vitoria and Chaz talking and laughing in Chaz's bedroom. And then she heard them make love. She cared for Sutt on Sunday morning. Vitoria and Chaz were sleeping, and Rita was out looking for food. Íso held Sutt and told him that she loved him. She pushed her forehead against his and she cried. He thought this was a game, and he punched at her and he laughed and then he pulled at her cheeks and her ears.

On Monday, when she met Eric, he said that he had had a dream and in that dream she was his wife and they lived on a lake and they had a large family. He said that there were children crawling and running everywhere. It was quite the life, he said, and he shook his head in wonder. He asked if a dream might indicate hope.

Oh, you stupid man, she thought. She knew that it was time. She held his hand. Oh, Eric, she said, that's a beautiful dream. She asked if he would meet her again on Wednesday.

Yes, he said.

Meja sat in her lap, looking out. She was barefoot on this day and Íso saw the fat lines on her ankles, and she touched Meja's toes, which were curled tightly with excitement. Her arms were strong, and her legs were strong, and she liked to stand on Íso's legs and do squats and test out her strength. This excited her and she smiled and spit and flapped her arms. She had no teeth, though her cheeks were a bit rough and Íso knew that this was a precursor to teething.

Of course she had great fear and doubts but then she pushed away her feelings and she went into that place inside of herself that was level and logical. She thought of Meja playing on the floor of the tienda, of Meja taking the boat across the lake to school, of Meja speaking Spanish, of Meja sitting across from her in their small kitchen. Meja's last name was Perdido, there was no other. She too dreamed. Of her mother. And of her father, who was long dead. In the dream about her father they were riding down out of the highlands towards the city in his van, just the two of them, and he was saying that it was necessary to grow a garden. Even a small one. He pulled packets of seeds from his pocket and placed them on the bench seat between them. Lima beans and radishes and maize and herbs of every kind. He said that they were hers to plant. And harvest. And then she woke up.

ON Tuesday evening, at the tenement, she washed all her clothes by hand and hung them on the balcony to dry. She wore one of Rita's shirts and a pair of Rita's pants, which were too large and made Chaz chuckle. Skinny as a dime, he said. She didn't pay him any attention, though she wanted to say that she had managed to gain five pounds. The week before, Rita had come home with a large backpack that she'd salvaged and Íso had asked if she might have it. She cut out the sides of the backpack and sewed in a mesh so that now the backpack had airflow. She had taken Sutt and placed him in the backpack, to see if he would fit. He did, though he struggled and cried. She'd pulled him out and held him and said, Oh, Sutt.

On her last night she was restless. She sat on the bed beside a sleeping Vitoria and she wrote a note to her, but when she reread it she realized that there was no explanation for who she was or for what she was about to do. And so she tore up the note. In the morning, when Vitoria left for Zone 7, Íso kissed her on both cheeks and said goodbye. She put on clean underwear and a clean button-down shirt and she wore jeans and socks and runners. She packed her bag. Formula and a few disposable diapers and baby wipes and a small blanket. Brushed her teeth and then packed her toiletries. The larger backpack was empty. She would carry that over one shoulder. She'd washed her hair the night before and it was shiny and clean and it smelled like lilacs. Chaz made mention of that. He liked to tell her sweet things, and she permitted him that. At noon, she told Rita and Chaz that she was taking a little trip, and she might be back, or she might not be. She gave them an envelope with her rent and food money. Chaz handed it back and said that she could use it more than they could. She hugged Rita, who cried a little. She buried Sutt's head against her chest and rubbed his hair. She kissed Chaz on the cheek and he looked right at her and said, Be safe.

She walked towards the city centre and took her regular buses to Zone 7. She arrived at Barbara and Chris's and she sat in the kitchen and looked out at the plants in the backyard while Champ played at her feet. She did not think. At 2:30 she left the dog locked up in the house and she walked towards the river and down the path and sat on the bench and waited. He came. He sat beside her. He took her hand. She looked at him and he looked at her.

You cut yourself shaving, she said. She touched the dried blood.

She asked if they might walk.

This was unusual and it made him anxious.

Come, just for a bit. She pulled him up. Meja was still in the stroller. She was covered with a blanket.

They stood and began to walk towards the footbridge, in the opposite direction from which he'd come.

He had both hands on the stroller and he released one and held it out to her and she said, Not here.

The stroller had a cover, a small awning that folded like an accordion, and she could not see the baby save for the blanket that covered her legs. Íso's arms ached. She was shaking.

He said that Meja was going for her inoculations today. Susan was taking her. His mind seemed clear.

You're having a good day, she said.

He said that he had woken up without the cloud.

He seemed wary, but he was also pleased to be with her. That she knew.

Beyond the bridge was a path that moved north into a cover of trees and she guided him in that direction. When they were beneath the trees, she took his arm and he touched his head to hers. A few hundred yards down the path they came to a bench and she asked if they could sit. He was more than willing. He was interested in her, in holding her hands, and touching her. She permitted this and she permitted him to kiss her. When he finally released her she stood and bent over the stroller and pushed back the top. Meja was awake. Her eyes were dark and large. Íso said, You. Meja made a face and pumped her arms and looked left and then right and then back at Íso. She reached deep into the stroller and gathered Meja up and there was a slight noise that came from her mouth, and Íso took Meja and held her.

She turned to Eric and clutched his elbow and squeezed it and she said that she was very happy. I'm in love, she said. She stood and laid Meja back in the stroller and took Eric's arm to pull him up.

He stopped her on the pathway and he held her. As always happened, he was unaware of time or space. He was also very strong, and if he had wanted, he could have squeezed the breath from her. She worked her hands up against his chest and pushed gently. He didn't let go. She said, Eric, you're hurting me.

Still, he held her.

She couldn't breathe. She said his name, sharply, and with her one free hand she began to hit him, across the back, the shoulder, his head. She hit his ear with her fist, and he grunted and released her and put his hand to his head.

I'm sorry, she said. Oh, Eric. And she took his head and she kissed the sore ear and she kissed his forehead and she smoothed his hair and she said again that she was sorry.

She took his arm again and said they should walk and not talk. They should appreciate each other. The outside. Listen, she said. Do you hear the birds?

He tilted his head and then shook it. He said that they should go back. It was time.

Up the path, in a clearing alongside the river, there was the public bathroom, and beyond the bathroom was another foot-bridge that led to the other side of the river. She saw the bathroom and the footbridge. She stopped and released Eric's arm and she bent over the stroller.

Then she stood up and said that the baby was dirty. She had to be changed. Come, she said, and she pulled him in the direction of the bathroom. As he trudged along beside her she told him that she would clean up Meja and then they would go back. Okay? She sat him on a bench and she leaned into him and she kissed him on the mouth and she said that he was a good man. You are good, she said.

~~~~~

HE watched her pick up the baby and walk towards the bathroom. He watched her walk around to the back of the building. He crossed his legs and listened. He thought he heard a bird. He turned his head to find the source of the bird sound but all he saw were leaves blowing in the wind. The wind was warm and the sun was hot on his head. He removed his scarf and folded it across his lap. The scarf was a burgundy colour and it went quite well with his grey slacks. His left shoe had a scuffmark, and so he took the burgundy scarf and he rubbed at the mark. The scuff had gone deep into the leather and any amount of rubbing was ineffectual. He had ruined a good pair of shoes. He laid the scarf again on his lap. He looked at his hands and thought he heard her voice. He looked up. She was still gone. He stood and walked towards the bathroom. He knocked on the women's door and called out. He pushed the door open and called out again. When he stepped inside he saw that the room was empty. He returned to the stroller and looked under the cover, as if he might be surprised by the impossible. He did a little skip, for he was anxious now, and he hurried back to the bathroom and looked again. Outside he called out, Hey, hey. And then he said Meja's name. He looked up at the trees and saw birds, and they were talking happily. He swivelled and saw the footbridge that led to the other side of the river. He walked halfway across the footbridge and then returned to the stroller. He walked in circles, calling out. He ran back to the bridge and called Meja's name over and over, but she was gone.

# 8.

SOUTHWEST OF KANSAS CITY, NEAR LEBO ON I-35, THERE
was a roadblock. From her seat, she saw the lights of the police cars
and she felt the bus draw to a stop. They waited. People grumbled.
Some stood to peer out into the darkness. The bus was not full.
She was alone at the rear. The driver opened the front door and
disembarked. He was talking. Someone else was talking. She
gathered up her backpack and she gathered up her baby and she
got up and stepped into the toilet and closed the door. She didn't
lock it. She sat down on the toilet lid and held her baby to her chest
and she breathed onto the baby's head and she whispered, It's okay,
it's okay. She heard a voice. It was moving towards the back of the
bus and she heard passengers talking, some female, some male,
and then it was quiet. She waited. Then a man's voice was right in
her ear, just outside the door, and he called out that he was going

to use the john. He laughed. Then there was a crackle of radio and an indistinct and rapid voice and she heard footsteps moving away. A siren sounded. Much later, the bus jerked, and it began to move. She stayed where she was. She took out a bottle that she'd prepared and she fed Meja as she sat on the toilet in the back of the bus. Meja fell asleep. Íso gathered up her things, and crept from the bathroom back to her seat. The bus was dark. A single light shone five seats ahead. Then the light went out.

THE day before, when she took Meja, she'd crossed the bridge at a fast walk, expecting Eric to call out immediately, but he hadn't. And then, once across, she'd turned left, away from the river and up towards the streets of Zone 7. She heard Eric calling then, and she began to run, her backpack banging, and she was talking to herself as she ran, and then she was crying, and she held the baby like a basket of eggs. At some point, right out there on the open street, she sat Meja on the sidewalk and she opened her backpack and slid Meja in. She barely fit. The hardest part was keeping the pack open with one hand while sliding Meja inside. Her legs kicked, and if one leg went in, the other wouldn't, and so Íso tried and tried again. Finally, Meja was inside. She thought it was a game. She chewed on the rim of the pack. She looked up at Íso and grinned. Íso whispered, It's okay, and she covered Meja's head and slipped on the backpack, heavier now, and as she walked, Meja seemed to calm down with the movement. It took her fifteen minutes to reach the gate and she passed through normally, even said good afternoon to the guard, and then she was out on the busy street. She stood at the bus stop and thought that she had five or ten minutes, and if a bus didn't come, she would have to walk or disappear. Meja was quiet. She had fallen asleep. When the bus arrived she climbed on and sat and looked out to the entrance of Zone 7 but all was calm. The guard was leaning against the fence and yawning. She got off the bus as they neared the downtown and she crossed the street on a green. She was not running now. She tried to hail a taxi, but several passed before one pulled over. The driver was older and when she told him that she wanted to go as far south as two hundred dollars would take her, he didn't seem surprised. He thought about this and he told her the name of a town. She asked if the bus, the Greyhound, stopped at that town. He didn't know. She told him to go. Take me there, she said.

You have the money? he asked.

She reached into her bag and showed him. And then she took Meja out of her backpack and held her to her chest. Meja was hot and she was whimpering. Íso took a bottle from the pack and laid Meja in her arms and offered her the bottle. She tasted it, and turned her head away. Began to cry. She wanted to sit up, and Íso let her, and so now she sat in Íso's lap and Íso pointed out the scenery passing by, but Meja was more interested in the necklace Íso was wearing. She tugged at the carving with its three petals. Touched it with great concentration. And then was tired of it. Íso tried to feed her again, and this time she accepted the bottle. Íso watched her mouth move. It was not a large mouth, but it took in the food in a large way. She marvelled.

The driver took her as far as Rochester, where he dropped her at the corner of 6th and 7th. She sat in a small café and ate an egg sandwich as Meja sat on the banquette beside her. She couldn't take her eyes off her, and even when she did, to take a bite of her sandwich, she felt that Meja might roll off the bench and under the table and disappear. She talked to Meja in her own language and Meja listened and leaned back, once again evaluating. She was guapa.

When she bought her ticket she had hidden Meja in her backpack because she didn't want people to know that she had a baby. And when she climbed onto the bus for Kansas City, Meja was again in the backpack. At the back of the bus, she took Meja out and fed her. No one on the bus knew that she had a baby. Meja didn't fuss or cry and she thought that she was very lucky.

She discovered that Meja was a fine eater. She liked to feed and then look around and then sleep. And then wake and stare into Íso's eyes. She rarely cried, except once when she had gas, and then Íso held her over her shoulder, face down, and bounced her lightly and the gas was released and Íso said, Good, good. And then she sat Meja on her lap and they stared at each other and made noises for each other and Íso studied every part of her child, from the top of her head to her toes. Her fingers were long and her feet were big. She would be tall, like her father, and she would have Íso's mouth and eyes. Íso spoke her name, Meja, and she sucked on Meja's fingers and she tried to teach her to say "mamá." She said "mamá" over and over again and Meja cooed at the sound and she cooed at the light touch of Íso's fingers dragging over her scalp. They were falling in love.

She had purchased a ticket that would take her through to Laredo, with transfers in Kansas City, Dallas, and San Antonio. At the bus station in Kansas City she had slipped Meja into the backpack and wandered around the station until she found a quiet corner, and only then did she take Meja out and feed her and change her. And hold her. Meja didn't seem to mind the confines of the pack, in fact she slept for the most part, and when she did wake and sputter a little, Íso swayed and hopped ever so slightly to keep her quiet. On the bus, Meja slept on her lap, and when she was awake, she stood on Íso's knees and Íso bounced her and spoke nonsense to her in her own language.

The countryside spooled out in a vista of forests and towns and cities and dried-out lakes and concrete and abandoned golf courses and graveyards of rusted vehicles and gas stations and vast fields of wheat and sorghum and corn in which an irrigation rig lay dormant and there were factories and warehouses and cars and trucks and great cities and intricately woven freeways that channelled those cars and trucks through those great cities and spit them out back onto the roads that intersected more fields of sorghum and soybean and in the morning when she woke, even though she had sworn that she would not sleep, she first located her baby and found her to be safe and asleep and then she looked out at that vista and saw the mist lying over the crops and a solitary tractor moving across a fallow field.

In that sleep that she had sworn she would not fall into she had dreamed and in her dreams that flickered and jumped she saw a wan woman floating in the waters at Ixchel and she saw the doctor

smiling and calling out to her and she saw a crop of children growing out of the earth with their faces turned towards the sun and
she saw her own child walk out of the field all bright and yellow
wearing a dress the colour of sunflower and she saw the boy lying
in the hollow she dug for him and at his head a spigot from which
water flowed and she stooped to drink from that spigot, her hand
resting on the boy's chest.

This was the dream she awoke from when the bus was stopped
at the roadblock. She realized immediately that she was being
hunted. Not she. The baby. One of those many cameras would
have picked up her image and it wouldn't be long now before she
was caught. Not long after the stop at the roadblock, at a place
named Emporia, she gathered her things and put Meja inside the
backpack and she disembarked and walked out into the country.
She would no longer trust the crowds, or the buses, or the places
where the cameras watched her. She would stay away from large
cities. She would walk on the less busy roads.

In the bathroom of a gas station, when she was alone, she laid
Meja on the counter and she washed her own hands and face and
then she took a paper towel and wet it and wiped at Meja's face
and hands. Her ears, her neck. Meja squirmed and turned away,
unhappy. She had run out of formula and had only one more
diaper, and she set out in search of a market. It was very hot, and
she thought that Meja would be suffocating in the backpack, and
so she found a quiet place by the doorway of a shop that cut keys,
and she removed her backpack and took out Meja, who was sweating. She carried her then, and when she found a drugstore and
entered, a current of cold air greeted them. She bought Pampers

and formula ready mixed and she bought wipes and she bought a chocolate bar and two bottles of water. Her budget had been altered by the cost of diapers and formula.

It was summer in America. August. The days and nights were still hot and this being so she found fields with tall crops where she made a nest amongst the sorghum or the wheat or the corn and she put Meja down on the backpack and she set herself down and in this manner they both slept. At night she woke and heard transport trucks gearing down on the interstate. The stars above were many. She felt safe. She had decided to give Meja the breast, even though she had no milk. She knew from observing other mothers with babies that it was possible to get milk flowing again, even with a six-month-old. It required patience. When Meja woke and fussed, Íso dribbled a little of the mixed formula on one of her nipples and she let Meja root. Which she did briefly, until the formula was gone, and then she fussed again. Íso dribbled on some more formula and brought Meja back to her nipple. Meja became frustrated and angry. She arched her back. Finally Íso gave her the bottle, and when she'd finished it, she put Meja's head against her bare breast and pushed her nipple against the baby's mouth. Now she didn't mind. Though she wasn't terribly interested. They lay like this, in the dirt, Meja's head against her bare breast, and in her sleep she turned towards the nipple. At one point Meja held the nipple in her mouth but didn't suck. Above them was the sky and beneath them was the earth. In the early light of the morning she again fed Meja, methodically adding formula to her nipple. And again Meja became frustrated. She even tried putting mashed banana on her nipple, but Meja turned away. She fed her the remaining banana. She laughed, and Meja laughed. The wind blew. A tractor passed nearby. She heard the tractor again later, coming nearer, and she stood and walked out of the cornfield past the farmer, who sat on the tractor and looked at her in surprise and then waved. He stopped the tractor and called out, but she ignored him and kept walking. On the shoulder now, heading south.

When the sun was high, she was thirsty, and she knew that if she was going to produce milk she would have to drink more water. Cars and pickups passed her by and everybody waved and she waved back. Late in the afternoon a red pickup approached from behind and as usual she stepped to the side and waited for it to pass, but this time the vehicle slowed and stopped. A man was at the wheel. A young boy sat in the passenger side. The boy lowered his window and the man leaned towards her. She stayed put, on the edge of flight, though there was nowhere to run.

You need a ride? the man asked. His vowels were flat and his consonants thick.

She shook her head.

It's mighty hot, the man said. We can help you to the next town.

She looked up the road and then looked at the man and she looked at the boy, and it was the boy who decided it for her. She stepped forward and the boy opened the door and then slid over. She climbed in. Meja sat in her lap. She shut the door.

The man idled back onto the road and picked up speed. He looked over at her and said that it was unusual to find a mother and a baby walking the roads out here. Are you lost?

She shook her head.

The boy held out his hand to Meja. Meja punched the air and squealed. The boy grinned.

What's his name? the boy asked.

It's a girl, she said.

What's her name?

Meja.

The giving of Meja's name had been spontaneous, almost prideful, and she thought that she had misstepped. But the man seemed unaware, and the boy was innocent.

Hi, Meja, the boy said. He touched Meja's cheek.

Where you headed? the man asked.

San Antonio, she said.

The man lifted his eyebrows. Said that she'd be lucky to get there by Christmas. That's a long walk.

I've got time, she said.

There was a Thermos on the dash and she'd seen it when she entered the truck and now she asked if they might have something for her to drink.

The man gestured at the Thermos and told the boy to give the lady some coffee. The boy scooted forward and reached for the Thermos and unscrewed the lid and then the stopper and he poured some liquid into the lid and held it out for her. She took it and drank. It was sweet and creamy and as she swallowed she felt the heat in her throat and then her stomach. She finished what the boy had given her and he asked if she wanted more.

If you have enough, she said.

Lots more where that came from, the boy said. He sounded like a little man.

They farmed twenty-five hundred acres of corn and sweet sorghum and wheat. They were Holdeman Mennonites and their family name was Wiebe. The father was Jasch and the mother Katerina. Six boys in the family, ranging from twenty down to seven. Knalls and Bient and Wellem and Johann and Franz and Josef. She learned all this at the supper table where she sat, the only girl save of course for the mother and Meja. The boys were all talkers except for Bient, who bowed his head and ate and snuck glances at her and then, when he received a smile from her, turned away red-faced. They ate homemade sausage and noodles with gravy, and they ate corn and fresh tomatoes with sugar sprinkled on top and sliced cucumber, and for dessert there was plum pastry. The food disappeared quickly, but not before a prayer, which was offered by Jasch. He thanked God for the sunshine and for the bountiful harvest and for the rains that hadn't come yet. He thanked God for the visitors, Íso and Meja, and he prayed that God might bless them and keep them safe from evil and that his face might shine upon them and give them peace, and he thanked God for the food and he asked for a blessing on the hands that had prepared it amen. All called out amen and then fairly flew at the food. The boys ate with gusto and when they were finished they all wanted to hold the baby, who was sitting in Íso's lap and pushing her hands into the cut-up spaghetti on Íso's plate and then shovelling it at her mouth. The gravy was thick and sweet. The oldest boy, Knalls, was the first to take Meja. He bounced her and chucked her chin and tickled her, and then Josef, the youngest and the one from the pickup, had a go and almost dropped her, and then the other three, and finally Bient, the quiet one, took her and sat on the couch and placed Meja at his hip and put his arm around her for protection.

We obviously need more girls around here, the father said. He wore a beard with no moustache and this made his face longer but she saw his mouth and it was kind. He winked at his wife, who shushed him. She turned to Íso and said that there was a bed for her for the night. Bient will sleep with his brother.

Katerina's accent was complex but Íso understood and she said that she had to go. Thank you.

You're not going anywhere, Katerina said. You have all day tomorrow and the next. San Antonio? My goodness. She said something in another language to one of her boys. The boy nodded and grinned at Íso.

She joined the family in the sitting room, for she had been invited, and they sat in a circle and listened as the patriarch read a long passage from the Bible and then there was a song, belted out with such great strength that she was astounded and for some reason overjoyed, and suddenly they were all on their knees with their heads pressed into the places where they had just been sitting, and she joined them, sat Meja on the soft chair and pressed her hands down onto Meja's legs, and in this manner, on her knees, she listened to the family pray, youngest to oldest, in a language that was unfamiliar, guttural, a singsong solo rising and falling, and the only indication that one had finished and the next would begin was a hearty amen that arrived as a shout, and it was like a dance where one steps into a circle as the others watch and nod, and steps out again to be replaced. Even Meja fell into the rhythm of the voices. She clucked and cooed.

And then they were standing and the older boys disappeared back out to the harvest. It was early morning when they returned. She heard them from her bedroom, talking in the kitchen. They were eating once more. And then gone again.

She had bathed the night before. Taken Meja into the bath with her and scrubbed her hair and ears and bottom and feet as she gurgled and spat and sucked on a washcloth. Then she'd plopped Meja on a towel outside the tub and quickly washed herself before Meja pulled her way across the floor towards the door. That night she tried again to breastfeed but Meja wouldn't latch. She kicked and fussed. There was no milk.

At the breakfast table there was Katerina and the youngest boy and Íso and Meja. Katerina asked if the baby was feeding.

She didn't understand at first and then Katerina pointed at one of her own breasts and asked again if the baby was feeding. The boy giggled. Íso said that she was trying, but she didn't have milk. Not yet.

Katerina didn't seem concerned. It will come, she said. Skin on skin is the best. Some honey on the nipple. Something sweet.

She spent that day at the farm. She felt safe. She had begun to see that the family had little interest in the outside world and that they were mightily independent. While Meja slept she picked beans in the garden with Josef, and Katerina made soup with potatoes and beans and sausage. Íso sat in a wooden lounger on the porch and gave a breast to Meja, who pulled at it half-heartedly. Katerina arrived and took the baby and disappeared. For an hour, before they went back out to the harvest, the boys played base-ball on the yard flanking the granaries. She stood in the outfield with Bient and after the game he brought her a cold glass of water. She thanked him. He said that he had built his own motorcycle. She asked to see it. The machine shed was cool and dim and it smelled of oil and gas and there were tools hanging on the walls and everything was ordered and clean. In the gloom he nodded at the bike and said it was a Norton 650. She learned that he would have to sell it because luxuries were not abided. He asked if he could take her for a ride. She told him that she was afraid of motor-cycles. He said that his mother said the same.

It so happened that she stayed the next day as well. It was Sunday, and the men didn't work. She joined the family at church. She rode in the pickup with Bient and Knalls, and she sat in the middle, holding Meja, while Bient pressed his leg against her thigh. She wore jeans. All the women in the church wore long dresses. The older women wore kerchiefs in their hair as well. She sat on the women's side, beside Katerina. The singing was again wonderful and again it carried her away. There was no piano, just the voices. Meja was adored. Íso was adored. Or so Katerina told her that afternoon. Everyone loves you, Katerina said.

Bient, who had taken to hovering, was at the table. His mother told him he could help Íso with the dishes. And so together they washed and dried the plates and cups, and poured boiling water over the cutlery. Bient asked her where her husband was. This was the first personal question she'd been asked. She said that there was no husband. Bient said that Meja must have a father. She said that there was a father, but he was gone. He nodded at this. He asked if she went to church. She said that her mother sometimes went to church. He said that she was very beautiful and that her hair was amazingly pretty. She thanked him and smiled. He asked if she wrote letters. She said that she could write letters. He was quiet, and then Josef appeared and wanted to show her his sunflower patch.

SHE left the following morning. Katerina gave her a ride to the nearest town. She advised against walking. It would be hot, what with the baby. She made Íso a lunch large enough to feed five. There was a bottle of water. Katerina had handed Íso her clothes, freshly laundered, and those shirts and pants that had holes had been mended with a fine stitching that was almost invisible. Katerina gave her a few small tops and shorts for Meja. When Íso said goodbye, Josef wanted to hold Meja one last time. Katerina hugged Íso and whispered in her ear. If there is danger, she said, walk the smaller roads. And do not trust strangers.

Íso said she would be careful.

Katerina said that she would pray for her. God keep you, she said. And she kissed the top of Meja's head.

Late that afternoon, on a rarely used side road, she found shade beneath a row of trees that produced a green fruit. She sat in the grass and unpacked the lunch. Ham sandwiches and raw celery and boiled eggs and cheese cut in chunks. There was a sauce made from crab apples for Meja and there was sliced watermelon and homemade yogurt with fresh raspberries. And a glass jar with cherry Jell-O that had gone to liquid but was taken greedily by Meja. Another glass jar, this one full of honey. After eating, Íso looked around to make sure she was alone and then she removed her top and lay on the grass and settled Meja on her chest and let her lie between her breasts. She noticed that one of her nipples was oozing a small amount of milk. She directed Meja's mouth towards her nipple. Meja tasted. Tasted again. And then latched. She didn't get much save the pleasure of the sucking, and the pleasure might have even been greater for Íso, who marvelled at the muscles of Meja's jaw. Good girl, she said, and she gave her the other breast and when she was finished, they lay side by side on the grass and they slept.

She woke to the sky above and she knew that she had never seen a sky so grand and so large and so deep, and she thought that God above must have great difficulty keeping track of his responsibilities, for even she, Íso, was overwhelmed by her one responsibility, Meja. She thought of her mother, and she anticipated her joy at seeing Meja. She worried for her mother's safety, but she knew that her mother had family and friends, and she knew that her tío, Santiago, would help. He would not let anything bad come to pass.

KATERINA had sewn a sling for the baby and in this way Íso could walk longer distances without her arms tiring. Katerina had provided a map as well, and marked out the smaller roads. Isó filled her water bottle at a Chevron station and purchased some food and walked out into the countryside and settled that night into another maize field. She ate a sweet bun that was dried out. Meja was breastfeeding well now. Íso had enough milk for three minutes on both sides. Then she fed her mashed banana. She'd run out of diapers and had taken to using cloths that Katerina had passed on to her. Done up with safety pins. She cleaned the cloths using the toilets and sinks of the gas station restrooms and hung them from her backpack to dry, or laid them atop cornstalks when she and Meja sat in the fields to rest.

She woke early and walked all that day. She found some cattails in the ditch and picked two and stuck them in the side pockets of her backpack. Late in the afternoon, the sky grew dark and it began to rain, a drizzle at first, and then it descended in black sheets. There was no shelter to be had and so she walked with her head down, covering Meja as best as possible.

A vehicle pulled up and stopped. The passenger door opened and a hand gestured. She looked inside but all she saw was the shape of someone, and because the rain was so relentless she made her decision and she climbed in and shut the door.

The man was alone. He was well dressed and he wore cow-boy boots and his hair was combed back and he wore a wedding ring. The rain fell slantwise. The wipers were frantic. The sky was black. Look at that mess, the man said. He reached into the back and fished for something and produced a hand towel, green, and offered it to her. Dry off that face, he said. And the baby. She obeyed. She wiped the water from Meja's head and then cleaned herself up and placed the towel on the bench between them.

The man put on music. He said that she was lucky. As was he. His voice was high and it had a timbre of surprise. He asked her name. She told him. He asked the baby's name. She told him. He touched the baby's head, by the crown, and she felt as if he had touched her without asking permission. He sang along to the radio and his voice was weak and she thought of all those boys singing in the sitting room of the farm where they had kneeled to pray. He said that he was delivering the Cadillac to a dealership in Tulsa. He said that she was a 1979 Eldorado. The car was wide and generous and all of leather and chrome and it was like a boat, and she knew that there was no way to leave the boat. She knew that she had made a mistake.

The man turned off onto another highway and she thought that they might be going in a different direction but she wasn't sure. She saw lights ahead and she said that she would stop there. She pointed. He laughed and said that there was nothing in that place, just a light indicating a spot on the ground. Not safe there, he said. They passed the light and she saw a farmyard and out-buildings and a farmhouse.

Take me there, she said. She was shaking, and she didn't want him to know, but she knew that he was aware, because her voice was tremulous.

He ignored her and turned off the radio. He said that she was young. Good thing I found you, he said.

She spoke then. She said that her child was very young and

she was tired and hungry and if he could take them to a nearby town she would pay him. She reached into her bag and took out her money wrapped in plastic and she held it up for him and said, Here, take it.

Don't want your money, he said.

He sang a little song then. She understood the words, she was not stupid. She knew English, even if the words were vulgar. And then he was singing the same words in Spanish, and she began to cry.

And she stopped. She picked up the towel and dried her tears and she looked at the man and saw his profile with his small chin and she said that she would do whatever he wanted. What do you want? she asked.

No no no no no. That's not how it works. What I want. What you want. In this you have no choice. When you climbed into my car you forfeited any choice. Sweet little Mexican wetback thinks she has a choice. No no no no.

I'm not Mexican, she said.

He laughed. He reached out with his right hand to stroke her face. I know you, he said.

She whimpered, and Meja began to whimper as well. He released her and she held Meja to her chest and whispered in her ear, Okay, okay.

His free hand lay on his thigh now and he drove with his left. Outside the rain was abating and only two vehicles had passed, a transport truck and a car, both heading in the other direction. The clouds scattered and the rain stopped, as if someone above had turned off the tap. The wipers squealed against the windshield.

They flapped on and on. The sun was in front of them to the west and it was bright red and it was setting and in another place it would have been beautiful. She saw the sky and the clouds moving above and the hedgerow to her right and a stand of dairy cows shouldered and circled as if in prayer. Meja slept. The man did not speak. Dusk came and she knew that she would die. And if this were to be, what would become of the baby? She said, Keep my baby safe.

He slowed the car and looked past her into a field where there was a lane. He picked up speed. Slowed again. In a world that asked for haste, he was unhurried. Time stretched out to infinity. He told her what he was going to do to her. He had a list. He laid it out for her in measured terms. He was an accountant tallying up his day's earnings. And for each number on that list, she said that she had a baby and could they drop off the baby in a safe place and then he could have her. You can have me, she said. But my baby.

You're a choir of one, he said. Sing on. He said that the baby was wanted, and that the baby had a price. The baby will be safe, he said. But you, you have little importance. No price.

He'd picked up speed again, but he was still looking for a spot, and she closed her eyes and opened them and she saw Meja on her lap. Look at you, she said.

When he slowed again, to a crawl this time, she opened the door. She heard him call out. The car stopped. Again he spoke, but she did not hear. She felt him reach for her but she was already outside and running down through the watery ditch and out into the field. She put her baby down in the dirt and the grain and she

ran in the opposite direction, out into the field of wheat that lay in
the dusk like a grey blanket over the earth.

BECAUSE it made life simpler, Sayed Kalif called himself Sami K.
He was a physicist, educated in England, and he'd worked for a
time with a research firm in Washington, DC. One day, driving
to work, he was pulled over by an unmarked police car. He was
blindfolded and taken to a building, unknown to him, where he
was interrogated and humiliated for three days. He was fed several bowls of soup during that time, a thin gruel with a few peas
swimming in the broth, and he was interrogated at random. He
was asked questions to which he did not know the answers, and by
the third day if he had been told what to confess to he would have
happily done so. And then he was released. Three months after he
had been taken, he quit his job and moved to Neodesha, Kansas,
where he purchased an abandoned homestead off Route 37. He
figured he had enough money in his bank account to last two years.
A creek bordered his land. The outbuildings and house were in
disrepair. At first he used water from the creek and then he hired
a driller, and after four attempts the driller struck water. Electrical
lines ran above ground from the hydro poles on Route 37, but he
foresaw a limited future and within six months he had set up an off-
grid solar power system. He patched the hardwood floors on the
main floor of the house. Painted. Repaired and shingled the roof.
There was a pot-bellied stove and from a stand of oak he selected
his trees and cut them down and worked them into eighteen-inch

logs that he split by hand and stacked by the shed, where they sat to cure for the cold days to come. He drove a Camino with no box, just the chassis, and he'd welded angle irons to the chassis and bolted in two sheets of plywood so that now he had a bed of sorts. He raised chickens for the eggs and killed the chickens when they stopped producing and with these chickens he made a broth that he poured into sealer jars and delivered to the neighbours around Drum Creek. A gesture of goodwill and peace, given to wary folks who were surprised to hear this trim, bearded dark-skinned man speak with an English accent.

On a Tuesday in late August he worked in his garden, digging up potatoes and carrots and picking ripe tomatoes. In the afternoon he drove to Coffeyville and picked up milk and bread and butter at the supermarket. At True Value he purchased 2 x 4 studs and framing nails and pink insulation and ten sheets of half-inch plywood, and he strapped this to the bed of the Camino and drove back to his land. Heading north on 169 he encountered a thunderstorm so fierce that he had to pull to the shoulder and wait it out. After it had passed he drove slowly, wary of his load and of the black puddles that caused his Camino to plane. It was dusk when he passed a car stranded on the far shoulder. No hazards. Long and boat-like. He slowed and then carried on. The car was an Eldorado, vintage, and it wasn't from those parts. He would have noted it previously. He slowed and pulled over. Made a three-point turn and drove slowly back towards the vehicle. His headlights revealed nothing save the empty car, slightly akilter on the shoulder. Nose pointing at the ditch. Passenger door ajar. He sat in the Camino and contemplated. The last light had just been siphoned from the sky. He exited and shut his door. Stood in the gloom. Heard a cat mewl out in the field. He approached the Eldorado. Looked out towards the field. Heard once again the cat, or some small animal. He had no interest in a confrontation, or trouble, or anything that might lead to trouble.

He looked into the passenger side of the Cadillac and saw a backpack and beside the backpack a baby bottle. He straightened and looked out again towards the field. Mosquitoes hovered near his neck and ears. The air was clean, there was a slight breeze, and he could smell clover. The cat mewled once again. He returned to his Camino and reached in behind his seat and pulled out a spade, a tool of cultivation, but it could be used for protection. He walked down through the ditch into the deep, wet grass and by the time he'd reached the wheatfield his boots and the cuffs of his pants were soaked. He went looking for the source of the cries and found a baby lying on the ground, nestled in the wheat. He stooped and picked it up. Wiped the tears off the baby's face. Held it. The baby was acquiescent and pushed against his chest. Thumped its legs as if it was incredibly happy to have found a human.

Who are you? he whispered.

Deeper in the field he heard voices, and he moved forward. He now carried the baby and he carried the spade, and so his hands and arms were full. The noises grew and he recognized them as human voices and he wondered if the baby was more important than the trek forward. He hesitated. He decided to lay the baby back against the softness of the grain. He did so. He built a little nest and made sure it was comfortable. And then he promised that he would return. The baby said nothing. Its eyes were dark and trusting.

He carried on, following the path of broken grain, and he came upon a man sitting astride a woman. He thought at first that they might be in congress, but they were fully clothed, and he saw that the man was rudely holding the woman and the things he said were rude and he heard her whimper, and then cry, and he saw that this was wrong, and so, fearing for his own existence, and aware of the baby back in the grain, he gripped the spade as if it were a baseball bat and he said, Look at me. When his voice was not heeded, he again said, Look at me, and as the man turned to look, he swung the spade at the man's head.

He didn't know what to do with her. He'd come to this land to escape, to settle and roost like an endangered species that senses the desire of others for its extinction and yet will struggle against that annihilation. He had been fervent in his privacy, and even the giving of gifts to neighbours—the broth from the boiled chickens, thick and lidded with grease—had been a gesture of separation. I will give, but not take. I come in peace. Leave me be. And now here she was, and he was at a loss. They had come up out of the field, running, she holding his hand and he holding the child. They'd left the man akimbo, groaning and mumbling, in the wheat beside the abandoned spade. The swing of the spade had been just hard enough to fell him briefly. A light knock. Sayed was not a violent man.

If she had not had the child he would have dropped her in Morehead, on the main street, or driven her to Coffeyville and booked a room for her at the inn. In the passenger's seat, she kept turning her head to look, as if expecting a following, and with each turn she moaned and then returned to her child and clutched at it. She wept grievously and her whole body shook and even after the weeping had halted she continued to shake.

He asked if that man was her husband.

She looked at him, dismayed. No, she said. No.

You didn't know him.

She shook her head.

He told her that she was safe. That no harm would come to her. But she seemed to be deaf, or not to believe. And so he took her home.


SHE slept in an old shed that he converted into a bedroom for her and Meja. There was a single cot and a small wooden table and two chairs and there were two windows that looked east towards the house where he lived. They did not eat together at first. He delivered food morning and evening, and if she was still sleeping, he left it on the stairs by her door. In the morning a plate of scrambled eggs or a bowl of Cream of Wheat, a pot of tea, a piece of bread and some jam. In the evening he might bring her fresh tomatoes and cucumber and a bowl of rice with a rich creamy sauce that was spicy and carried heat, a flavour unlike anything else she had tasted. It was delicious. Or one time, baked quartered potatoes that tasted of lemon and rosemary. Baked tomatoes as well. She was allowed to use his bathroom and shower, but only when he was not in the house. The same rules applied to his kitchen, but because he cooked for her, she had no reason to use the kitchen. His existence might have been perceived as meagre, if she hadn't known this kind of reality back in her own village. He spoke little, and when he did speak, it was to offer instruction, or to ask if she was okay. She was. He was very fond of Meja and he took to touching Meja's head or clutching Meja's fist and speaking to her softly. In those moments she saw the kindness in his eyes.

In her nightmares the man killed her, and she woke, horrified, and she lay panting and soaked in sweat. In another she killed him, and bit out his tongue and spit it on the ground. Horrifying as well. And when she woke she touched herself to verify her own existence and she realized that she was alive, and safe. As was Meja, lying by her side. They were in a bed with clean sheets, and the room had a padlock. Sami had shown her how to use it, and so each night when she retired, she slipped the lock into place and slept with the key beneath her pillow.

She heard him talking one morning, when she had risen early and gone outside her hut to walk with Meja. She asked him about this later in the day, and he paused and said that he had been praying. He prayed five times a day—three times silently, two times out loud. He asked if she prayed, and she said that she did.

The first time he left to get supplies, he told her to stay out of sight, and he said that if anyone should come, she was to remain invisible. When he used the word "invisible," she thought that he was right. She wanted to be invisible.

When he worked in his garden, she helped as Meja sat on a blanket between the rows of tomatoes. And then Meja was crawling along the rows and reaching for the bright fruit. He thought this was delightful. Let her, he said, whenever Íso tried to save the tomatoes from Meja's grasp. In the mornings she gathered eggs and delivered them to his kitchen. When he slaughtered a few chickens, she helped with the plucking and evisceration. She chopped wood. She asked if she might keep his house clean, and he said that she wasn't his maid. She said that she had to earn her keep. He said that she had nothing to earn.

And then one day, three weeks into her stay, he invited her to join him for the evening meal. Please, he said, come.

His table was set with two plates and two glasses, and beneath the cutlery there were napkins made of cloth that he had folded. She sat and held Meja, who promptly grabbed a spoon and banged it against the wood of the table. She took the spoon away.

It's okay, he said. Let her make music.

She gave the spoon back and the banging continued.

He served a chickpea dish cooked with peppers and onions and he ladled this on top of rice. They drank water. She ate and said that it was very delicious. She set a few chickpeas on the table for Meja, who picked them up carefully and ferried them to her mouth and chewed happily.

He asked what her plans were.

She looked at him and said that she would leave the next day.

Is that what you think I want?

You've given enough.

How much is enough?

She looked down.

He asked where her husband was.

There is no husband.

He was quiet. And then he asked after the father.

She did not answer.

He asked her if she had been heading north or south when he'd found her.

South, she said.

Are you in danger? he asked.

She said that she might be.

Meja is yours, he said.

Oh, yes. Yes. She's mine.

I'm sorry, he said. It's not my affair.

She said that it was okay. He had a right. She was his guest.

She stood and handed Meja to him. He took Meja and sat her on his lap as Íso cleared the table and washed the dishes. She was aware of him watching her as she worked.

He said that he was surprised sometimes at the cruelties men were capable of. And then he said that he shouldn't be surprised, for he was a man as well.

But not cruel, she said.

Everyone is capable, he said.

She shook her head and turned to him and said, I don't think so.

They began to share evening meals at his kitchen table. And

then breakfast as well. He liked to scramble eggs with red peppers and onion and he liked a little honey with the eggs. She did the same. Meja especially enjoyed the honey. Sayed sometimes played cuckoo with Meja, hiding his head under the table and then popping up. Meja was terribly pleased with this game.

One morning he asked her where her home was. She told him. He asked if she was returning home and she said yes.

You'll have to cross the border into Mexico, he said.

Of course.

Do you have papers?

She shook her head.

And Meja?

No.

It will be difficult.

I know, she said. But I came here without papers, and I'll return without papers.

The following day he drove to Coffeyville to buy supplies. She washed her clothes and she washed Meja's clothes and diapers and she hung everything in the sunshine, on the line behind her shed. She cleaned his kitchen. Washed her hair. She stood in the doorway of his bedroom, but she did not enter. He was very neat. And he had very few things. He did not smoke or drink and he prayed often and he read his holy book and he sometimes didn't eat for religious reasons. In the afternoon heat she and Meja lay on their bed in the coolness of the shed. Meja slept. A fly buzzed against the window. Íso heard a car and then the car stopped in the yard and a door opened and shut and she heard footsteps on the gravel. She rose and stood at the window and looked out into the yard. She saw a police car and she saw a state trooper walking the perimeter of the yard. The trooper walked up the stairs to the door of the house and knocked. Waited. Then he descended the stairs and disappeared around the side of the house. She waited. He reappeared eventually and walked over to his car and looked about one last time and then climbed in and left. She sat down and breathed.

That night at supper she told him about the police car and she said that she would be leaving.

He didn't seem surprised. He asked how she would travel.

She said that she might go by bus. Or walk. Or catch rides.

I don't think so, he said. She was quick to look up at him but he wouldn't allow her to speak. He said that he would drive her to the place she wanted to go.

She said that it wasn't safe for him. She said that Meja was hers, but others didn't think so.

And she told him. About Meja's birth and how she was taken. And she told him about crossing the border into America and she told him about Gabriel and about Gabriel's mother and she told him about Saint Falls and finding Meja and she told him about the doctor and she said that though he was the father he wasn't really a true father and she said that she had taken her baby back in order to return to her own place. When she was finished speaking he said nothing for a long time. Meja fussed and she lifted her top and offered her a breast. She had never done this before in front of him but at this point he didn't notice. Or if he noticed, he didn't think it remarkable. Or it was very remarkable and he was willing to accept its importance. He looked only at her face. He said that none of this surprised him. He was aware of the world out there. They are looking for you, he said.

Not me. The baby.

You both.

I did nothing wrong, she said. I only took my baby.

You have no proof that she is yours. No papers.

I have my genes. My DNA. That's proof.

You have no power, he said.

Will you report me? she asked.

No. No. He said that he would have acted as she had. But that he would have had different motives. He could not imagine giving up a child to be raised in a world of unbelief. A heathen world. Her motive was maternal. His would have been religious.

You think I'm sinful, she said.

It doesn't matter what I think, he said.

She said that she was aware of her wrongdoing when she took Meja. And that there would come a day when Meja would ask who her father was. And she would have to explain. A child is not an object that you cut in half and then each takes a share, she said. A child is unaware. She has no choice. This city, this country, this mother, this father. It's fate.

Meja's fortunate, he said. She's deeply loved.

Meja sat up quickly and looked directly at him when she heard him speak her name. She grinned. Closed her eyes coyly. Tilted her head.

She likes you, Íso said.

She knows me.

They left that night. She packed her few belongings and, as he had advised, left no trace of their stay. They drove south into the darkness and he detoured the nearby towns and by dawn they were well through Oklahoma and beyond Dallas. He pulled into a rest stop north of Waco, where she used the washroom, and they sat in the car and ate cold sandwiches he'd picked up at a gas station. Egg salad and pickles. She'd slept most of the night, waking every so often to ask him if he was sleepy, and then falling asleep again herself, the memory of his profile in the glow of the dash a strange comfort. She didn't know him truly. But she did know that she could trust him. And that was enough. She had no fear of him. He was like a brother, though the one time she told him this he said that he was not her brother and he was so adamant that she wondered if she'd upset him. And she let it go.

HE dropped her off in Laredo in the early afternoon. On a side street near the Lincoln Port of Entry. They sat for a time. He'd turned off the engine and it ticked as it cooled. He asked her how she planned to cross. She said that she would manage. He said that there must be other ways of crossing. She had to be careful. She said that she'd come this far and she had no plans to get caught and sent back. She'd gathered her bags, one of which held fresh diapers and formula and several bananas and a sandwich that he'd bought for her at their last stop. She clutched Meja.

He asked if she wanted his help.

I'll be fine, she said, though she was completely uncertain. Fearful.

She opened the door.

He reached out a hand to shake hers. She took his hand and then with his other hand he touched Meja's head. Go with God, he said.

Thank you, she said. And she climbed out.

When he was gone, she stood on the sidewalk and waited, perhaps hoping for him to return, or perhaps hoping for a miracle. Nothing. She and Meja were alone.

She did not know how she would cross the border at Laredo. She had no papers, and she was in possession of a child who had no papers. At that time the border was sealed one way, the way into America, and it was a known fact that you could walk across the border from Laredo into Nuevo Laredo and arrive in Mexico without papers, though it was also known that you could be arrested for making that mile-long walk. For any reason. Perhaps for the look of the clothes you wore, or the tilt of your head, or the length of your hair. It was rumoured that pretty girls were stopped and interrogated and searched, simply because they were girls, and pretty, and alone. Or not alone. Perhaps there might be three girls, but they would still be searched. There were no rules. No abiding guidelines. Everything was possible, and sometimes nothing was possible. These were the rumours.

In a small park off Farragut Street, she shared a banana with Meja. Nibbled at her sandwich. Everyone she heard now spoke Spanish and she felt safer, though she knew that this wasn't necessarily so. She walked south on Santa Maria Avenue until she arrived at a park that bordered the Rio Grande. She sat, holding Meja, and she looked across the river to Mexico. Just over there. A black boat flying an American flag moved past slowly. Two men holding rifles in the bow. There was a man playing football in the park with two young boys. She watched them until they left.

She walked up to the Lincoln Port of Entry and watched the pedestrians cross over into Mexico. Most were carrying bags or backpacks and were in larger groups. There were very few solitary travellers. She approached a young woman sitting on a bench with her two children and she excused herself.

Is it safe? she asked. To cross the border?

The woman looked at Íso, and she looked at Meja, and she said that it was always easier to get out than it was to get in. She gestured at Meja and asked, This is yours?

Íso nodded.

What's her name?

Íso told her.

The woman repeated Meja's name and she introduced herself and she introduced her young boy as Rodrigo and she held up her infant and said that her name was Ana. She said that it was very little problem if you had nothing to hide. Most just walk through. If you have a backpack, like yours, they will inspect it. Do you have papers for the child? she asked.

Íso shook her head.

Then they won't let you pass. Your child must have papers. Sometimes you can buy papers but it is much.

Íso asked if there was another way.

The woman said that there were sometimes boats. North of Eagle Pass. She should ask for a boat ride. Those were the words. A boat ride.

Íso thanked the woman, and she said goodbye to the children. She stood off to the side, under the awning of a leatherworks stand, and she watched the woman and her children cross over a long concrete walkway that was walled on both sides. They passed through a turnstile and walked some more, and then disappeared.

COMING into Eagle Pass by bus she remembered her earlier crossing and she remembered the desert and she remembered the boy. She pushed away her thoughts. She left the bus station and walked up North Adams to the Rio Grande café and ordered scrambled eggs and juice and she fed some of the egg to Meja, who happily received the food. Offered her a little orange juice as well. Cleaned her with a napkin. She wandered the streets with Meja in the sling, talking to her, telling her that all would be good. She sang for her, softly. She did not know how to find the right people. She had no idea who the right people might be. On a bench, close to the public library, she sat and watched the pedestrians and the cars passing by. Late in the afternoon, having traversed much of Eagle Pass, she found a fruit stand just off the main street, and she bought freshly cut papaya and half a lime and she ate the papaya and sucked on the lime as she squatted in the shade, Meja in her lap. She fed tiny pieces of the papaya to Meja. Men passing by looked at her in great detail and she felt their eyes on her body, but she did not look into their eyes, and she pretended to herself that she was alone in a vast field of sunflowers and that nothing could touch her. A police car moved by slowly and she looked away and realized that she should stay off the streets. She prayed for herself and she prayed for Meja, and when she looked again the police car had moved on.

She took a room that she could not truly afford, at a motel where the desk clerk was a young woman who spoke Spanish. Íso paid up front. She studied the young woman's face and then decided to take a chance and she said that she wanted a boat ride.

The young woman didn't even look at her. She turned to the cash register and then took a key and handed it to Íso and told her the room number. She said nothing more.

Íso fell asleep immediately, Meja at her side, and she woke to the phone ringing. She knew no one who might call her, and she stared at the phone for the longest time before she picked it up.

Yes? she said.

You're looking for a boat ride? a man's voice said.

Yes.

How many?

Only me. And my baby.

So two.

My baby's young.

Three hundred, the man said.

I have only two hundred.

There was silence. Then the man said that he would pick her up at the motel the following evening at 8 p.m.

She spent the night sleeping and then waking and listening to voices in the parking lot, and she heard arguing, and then the roar of a pickup, and finally silence. She got up and laid her remaining money on the bed and by the light of a small lamp she counted three hundred and thirteen dollars. She separated out two hundred and put the rest inside her top, tucked beneath her bra. This had been her life over the past months, and she was not yet finished with it. She was very tired.

She slept and Meja woke her with hungry cries. She fed Meja. Cut open an avocado and pushed a little of the meat into Meja's mouth. She spit it out and cried. She walked Meja back and forth, jostling her, sitting down to offer a breast, but Meja wasn't interested. She was drooling and rubbing her mouth and blubbering a lot. She tried again with the breast and this time Meja accepted it. Íso told her that she was a girl most delightful and most smart and most beautiful.

She kept off the streets the following day, spending time at the library and walking through the malls and by evening her feet ached. Meja was fussy. Again she drooled and rubbed at her mouth. At 8 p.m. Íso stood in the shadows of the entrance to the motel and she watched. A white pickup pulled into the parking lot and sat for the longest time. Then the door to the pickup opened and a young man in a cowboy hat exited. He gestured for her and she stepped out of the shadows and approached. He indicated that she should get into the pickup, and that she should crouch on the floorboard. She looked around and she looked at the man and she thought that if she got into the truck she might disappear along with her baby and no one would ever know. She was helpless. She climbed into the pickup and crouched amongst the garbage on the floor. Empty beer bottles and discarded fast food wrappers and cigarette butts. There was not enough room for both her and Meja, and so she sat Meja on the seat and clamped her there. The young man did not introduce himself, nor did he speak. She could smell him, a sharp scent of old sweat. He started the pickup, reversed, and shifted into drive. He turned on the radio and found a country music station and he rolled down his window and lit a cigarette. Íso had one hand on Meja, and she pressed the other against the dashboard. She kept her eyes lowered. Meja tried to stand and hold the man's shoulder. She used his shirt to draw herself up. Íso pulled her back down and told her that it was quiet time. Shhhh, shhhhh, she said. Meja imitated her and put her finger to her mouth. The man ignored both Meja and Íso, though he didn't seem to mind Meja pulling at his shirt. At some point he reached over and turned off his headlights and he slowed down and he swore occasionally as the pickup found a rut, or slid sideways. She did not like the man.

The boat was at the water's edge and it was very small. It had no motor, just two oars and a place for six people. There were four men and Íso, and there was Meja and there was the skipper. She paid the driver of the pickup and he counted the money by touch, or perhaps he was able to see in the dark. When he had finished counting he folded the bills and slipped them into his pants pocket and gestured at the boat. He climbed back into his pickup and drove off into the darkness.

She entered the boat. No one spoke. As they crossed, she heard the dipping of the oars in the water and the breathing of the man who was carrying them across. And then Meja began to fuss and the skipper called in a soft voice for silence. Íso was sitting across from a boy, not more than sixteen, who was watching her. She didn't want to but she opened her blouse and offered Meja a breast. The boy watched. Meja latched and then leaned back and reached with her near hand and held it out to the boy. The boy took Meja's hand and called her guapa but he was looking directly at Íso. Íso wanted to turn away, but she didn't.

When the boat hit the mud and sand of the far shore, the men scrambled and the boat rocked and Íso sat holding her child, afraid that she would be tossed into the water. The man who had skippered the boat asked for Meja and Íso handed him the child without thinking, and then panicked. But he stepped off the boat onto the shore and he held out a hand for Íso and she accepted. When she was on shore he gave her back the child.

Thank you, she said. Thank you.

You are in Mexico, he said. And then he said, Go, and she went.

The boy on the boat had eyed her the whole time. Even when he held Meja's hand, he had eyes only for her. They had been facing each other, their knees had touched, and he had not taken his eyes off her even though she had given him every reason not to look. She snuck glances, but he was still focused on her. She was terrified. She'd held the baby up for him to see, as if to say, I am a mother, but he ignored the baby. On the shore now the young man was beside her and then he was behind her. It was dark and there were no lights, only the young man and her and Meja. She heard the voices of the other men who had been on the boat and she called out and said, Please. Hello, please. I'm here, she said. Please. She ran in the direction of the voices and she came upon the men and asked if she might stay with them. They were indifferent. As they walked, the younger man followed from a distance. She did not know if three men were safer than the one boy, but she thought that one out of three might have a heart, or a code that he lived by. She was taking a chance.

She spent the night with the three men in a covey of trees, where a fire was built. She had no food, but one man, the oldest, offered some of his portion, and she took it and said thank you. Beans and tough beef in a cold burrito. She chewed slowly and when she was done she again said thank you. The oldest man asked her where she was from. She told him. She asked him where he was going, and he said that he might go anywhere. He had no home. When she changed Meja, she turned away from the men and laid a small blanket on the ground and then crouched over Meja so that the men could not see. She tried not to sleep. And when she slept, she woke and was distraught that she had slept. The boy, the one on the boat who had touched knees with her and watched her with such greed, was out there in the darkness somewhere. She was cold and Meja must have been cold as well, because she was restless and kept waking. She sat cross-legged by the dying fire and held Meja close and offered the warmth of her skin. Meja fed and eventually slept.

In the morning, she rose and gathered up Meja. The oldest man was awake, squatting by the dead fire, and she asked him the direction of the road. He pointed and said that it was an hour from this place. He did not ask if she wanted help or if she wanted to stay or if he might walk with her. He sat on his haunches in the cold air and lit a cigarette and watched her and he told her that the danger in this place was not heat, or thirst, or snakebite, but young men who looked for girls like her.

I have a baby, she said.

He said that the baby meant nothing. He was very matter of fact. She thought that he was not a dangerous man, or he would not be saying these things.

They said goodbye and she walked through the scrubland and the desert until she came to the road. There was very little traffic and when a vehicle finally approached she turned and she waved, but the vehicle passed on. Two hours later she was still walking when a pickup pulled over and idled on the shoulder. A motorcycle was tied to the bed of the pickup. A man sat at the wheel, and he called out through the open passenger window that she should get in. She looked at him and saw that he was very old and this gave her heart and so she obeyed. She climbed up into the cab and settled Meja on her lap and she said, Thank you.

The man clutched and shifted and pulled out onto the highway. He did not speak for the longest time, and she was grateful, though she felt, as usual, a twinge of dread.

And then he said that he was going to Saltillo. And you? he asked. She told him.

He said that it was a great distance, but that she was heading in the right direction.

He was a small man, and sitting at the wheel he looked dwarfed and she thought him harmless, but she knew that what might appear to be harmless wasn't always so. He said that his name was Eduardo.

She told him her name and she told him Meja's name.

He said that it was a pleasure. He asked if she was hungry.

She said that she was.

And the baby?

She's always hungry.

We will eat, he said.

I don't have any money, she said.

He lifted his shoulders and said that it wasn't necessary.

They stopped at a roadside restaurant. He ordered two plates of huevos rancheros and two coffees and he ordered porridge made of rice for Meja. Eduardo drank coffee and he looked at Íso as if seeing her for the first time and he said that she was very young.

She had no answer for what was true.

He said that he had a grandson who lived in Saltillo, and the motorcycle in the bed of the pickup was for the grandson. I spoil him, he said.

His hair was very black for an old man and it was combed back and he had deep lines on his forehead and on his face and Íso found him to be very handsome. When the food arrived they did not speak, but ate with great concentration, even Meja, who sat in Íso's lap and accepted the rice gruel she offered. Íso had added sugar and a little milk, and checked the temperature beforehand. Meja ate quickly and with pleasure.

He dropped her off at the bus station in Saltillo. He gave her a little cash and she took it without shame and said thank you. He asked if he could hold the baby. She handed Meja to him and he took her and cradled her and then kissed the top of Meja's head as if blessing her.

He gave the baby back and said that she was a good mother. He wished her safe travels. And then he left her.

I⊤ took her five days to cross Mexico via the coastal route. She rode local buses during the day and for the first two nights she took cheap rooms. In Tampico she found a small cold-water closet for ten dollars and she bathed Meja with a rag and she fed her and she laid her down to sleep on the single bed and then she showered and washed her hair with a small piece of soap and then she sat on the edge of the bed and she ate tortillas and a piece of corn brushed with chilies. When night fell, she stood in the darkness of her room and looked out the window onto the street below and she watched men in pickups and cars carry away the girls who walked the sidewalks. Young girls. Older women. All willing. At night, she woke and heard shouting from the room next door, and then came the sound of glass breaking and a woman crying, and out in the hallway there were shouts of glee or sorrow, she could not tell, and in the street below there was much to be heard, and she covered Meja's ears and smelled Meja's head. She decided then that the bus was a safer place. And so, in the days to come, she kept moving, sometimes standing for hours as she held Meja. With a serape purchased in a market in Ciudad Victoria, she had fashioned a more comfortable sling for

Meja, and in this way she managed to sleep for brief moments as she stood on the swaying bus, her legs aching, but always she counselled herself that she was young and she was lucky, and sometimes she was lucky enough to have a man offer up his seat to a young woman holding a child. She was favoured. She was unknown. There was no curiosity about her, and she took comfort in her anonymity. The world she had left behind became as a dream, a fantastical world out of which she had risen. She felt very strong.

Two days later, ten quetzales remaining in her pocket, she rode up out of San Lucas Tolimán in the back of a pickup surrounded by her people and she saw the sun falling over the lake and she saw the fishermen in their cayucos and she smelled the smoke from the maize fields high in the hills. Descending onto a flat plain where the road ran through a coffee finca she felt the wind that came off the lake, the wind that removed all sin, and she ducked her head and whispered in Meja's ear that they were home.

# 9.

The lake at Ixchel, situated along the Sierra Madre de Chiapas, is the deepest lake in Central America. In the middle of the last century, the government, hoping to attract tourists, specifically anglers, introduced a foreign fish, the black bass, which ate the native fish and contributed to the extinction of a water bird called the Atitlán Grebe. No one speaks anymore of the Atitlán Grebe, save for those fishermen who are in their later years, or a few souls who study birds and are inclined towards preservation. The Atitlán Grebe had slate-grey legs, and a bill with a bold black vertical band. It was rather nondescript. It had small wings. It was flightless.

Three days after the kidnapping of the doctor's child in Saint Falls, about which the village knew nothing, a stranger had arrived at the hotel near the clinic at Ixchel and introduced himself as an amateur birder. He spoke of the Atitlán Grebe and he mentioned two other birds, the Horned Guan and the Azure-rumped Tanager, two endangered birds found in the cloud forest above the lake. He hoped to sight one of these birds, or hopefully both. This stranger was seen in the pueblo, always walking, wearing his Tilley hat, and carrying his binoculars. He spoke a rudimentary Spanish. He handed out candies to the local children. He asked a few questions here and there about Señora Perdido and her daughter, but the answers he received were vague and contradictory. The mother used to have a daughter but she was now gone. Or the daughter had died travelling to America. Or the daughter had returned but was now working in Guatemala City, as a nurse, or a doctor. Or she was studying at the university. He went to the clinic and spoke with the director, Elena. She was quite beautiful, and very willing to answer his questions, and of course she knew the doctor and his wife, and she said if she heard anything about the child she would contact him immediately. They sat in chairs, facing each other, and he was aware of her dark blue dress and her pearls and the colour of her skin and he felt a stirring of desire. She leaned forward and said that he shouldn't expect anything to be simple. This is not a simple place. One doesn't fly down here and find a child that has been kidnapped. A child that in fact belongs to the woman who took her.

I think we can agree that she gave it up, he said.

She might not agree.

Who can I trust? he asked. The police?

She smiled. This is not America, she said.

He stood and reached out a hand. She took it and held it. He thanked her. And she thanked him. They agreed to keep in touch. He left the clinic and walked back to his hotel, aware of the heat from the sun on his back. He was distracted, and he knew that it was not a good thing to be distracted.

The following day he visited the tienda of Señora Perdido and observed her talking to customers. He did not approach. He just observed. Late that afternoon he drank a Gallo beneath the hotel gazebo. He had yet to take a trip into the cloud forest in search of the rare birds.

And then he disappeared for a time. Rumour had it that he had gone back to his home, or to the city to speak to the authorities, or perhaps he himself had been robbed by ladrones and left by the roadside to die. This was wishful thinking.

When he returned three weeks later, he could not be missed as he strode along the small lanes of the village, or as he folded himself into a tuk-tuk. He again took a room at the same hotel.

On a Saturday, the stranger once again entered Señora Perdido's tienda. She was alone at the counter. The stranger walked about, looking at the wares. He opened the fridge and inspected the butter and the yogurt. He hefted the bread. He stepped out under the awning and looked down and then up the street. Finally, he returned and he traversed the floor and stood before Señora Perdido.

Señora Perdido smiled at him. She wished him a good afternoon.

On this day the stranger was dressed not in his birding gear, but more formally. He wore a white shirt and black pants and he wore polished leather boots. To Señora Perdido he resembled men she had met before, perhaps even a younger version of Lewis, the man who had been her teacher so many years ago in San Francisco. Or he might have resembled the men who came to her tienda as missionaries, usually young men in dress slacks and white shirts and ties who spoke broken Spanish and wanted to make her a happier person. The stranger had the look of an evangélico, of a man who knew what he believed and was astounded that others did not agree. In any case, the stranger stood before her.

He said, My name is Derek Grima. Íso Perdido. She is here?

He was speaking his high school Spanish.

There is no Íso here, Señora Perdido said.

Not here?

Señora Perdido shook her head.

There is a baby. I am looking for the girl called Íso, and the baby called Meja. They are together.

Señora Perdido bowed her head.

The man asked in English if Señora Perdido spoke English.

In Spanish she said that she spoke Spanish.

The man looked around the shop. He reached into his pocket and took out a photograph. It was a photo of Doctor Mann and his wife. He laid the photo on the counter and asked if Señora Perdido knew these people.

Señora Perdido leaned forward and studied the photograph as if it were an ancient artifact. She excused herself and went to the back and returned with her reading glasses and leaned once again towards the photo. This one, she said. That is Doctor Mann.

You know him? the man asked. His voice was a little higher in pitch.

Of course. Everyone knows Doctor Mann.

He is a friend of your daughter's?

Everyone was Doctor Mann's friend. Señora Perdido lifted her arms as if to envelop all of humanity. He was loved, she said.

Your daughter Íso too?

The nurses, the keepers, me, the other doctors. Everyone.

Señor Grima leaned back from the counter. He sighed. He retrieved the photograph, slipped it into his front pocket, and said in his simple way, We come back.

Señora Perdido nodded. Okay, she said. You come back. Her voice was shaking, but the man did not notice.

When the stranger had gone, Señora Perdido closed her tienda, put on a jacket, and stepped out into the street and waved down a tuk-tuk. Her heart was both light and heavy. If she were to cry, though, it would be from relief and happiness. She directed the driver to take her to the carpintería, on the other side of town. She found Santiago staining a massive door that had been laid out on sawhorses. His hands and fingers were brown and the air smelled of the fumes from the oil. Santiago laid down the cloth and offered her a stool. She refused. She told him about the stranger. Santiago nodded and said that he was aware. She said that the man had been in the tienda and he had shown her photos of the doctor and his wife. And he'd asked about the baby, and he'd asked about Íso.

Santiago stepped sideways and picked up his cloth and bent to inspect the wood. He rubbed at a spot and then looked up and said that she should not worry. It will be fixed, he said.

Íso has the child, she said.

Yes, Santiago said. She has the child.. He smiled. His eyes creased. And she will keep the child.

THE stranger returned to Señora Perdido's tienda the following day. He had with him a young man who would act as his translator. A man Señora Perdido did not know. A man who was from else-where. Also a stranger.

The translator introduced himself as a friend of Señor Grima's. His own name was Pedro. He would translate. Okay?

Señora Perdido said that he could do as he pleased, but there was nothing new to say.

Pedro spoke with Señor Grima. They conferred in whispers. Pedro lifted his head and said that Señor Grima was looking for a child by the name of Meja. A child who belonged to Doctor Mann and his wife. There was reason to believe that Señora Perdido's daughter, Íso, was in possession of Meja. Señor Grima has come to return the child to the doctor and his wife, Pedro said.

There is no child here, Señora Perdido said.

If not here, then where?

Nowhere.

The men conferred some more. Pedro lifted his head and said that the child would be found. It was just a matter of time. Señor Grima thinks that you are not telling the truth, he said. It was clear that he was not happy to speak these words—in fact, he seemed to understand that he might have chosen poorly in taking this job of translating.

Señora Perdido sensed Pedro's hesitation, and she saw that she held a certain advantage, no matter how weak. She told Pedro that it was dangerous for Señor Grima to be looking for something that was not his. She said that Señor Grima should return to his own country. It was safer there.

Do you want me to tell him this? Pedro asked.

Señora Perdido shook her head. Tell him that I'm a simple woman who runs a tienda, and if he would like some butter or bread, I have that. Otherwise, I have nothing. He's knocking on the wrong door.

Pedro translated.

Señor Grima spoke to Pedro. He was angry, but he spoke calmly. He said that the mother was making a mistake. A dangerous mistake. And that she would have to open the door.

Señora Perdido understood English, of course. She stood, and she began to speak English to Señor Grima. She said that it was he who was making a dangerous mistake and that there was no door to open.

Both men were surprised by this outburst and Señora Perdido was immediately sorry that she had exposed herself in this way.

Pedro said, You speak English.

I do, Señora Perdido said.

Then why am I translating? Pedro asked.

Because it's your job, Señora Perdido said. She shrugged.

Pedro turned to Señor Grima and said that they would now go. Señor Grima protested.

We will go now, Pedro repeated, and he took Señor Grima's arm and led him out into the street.


DEREK Grima disliked tropical countries. The vegetation was overwhelming, there was no such thing as dusk, the dogs were ill fed, most people were shorter than he was, the garbage on the streets disturbed him, and inevitably there was the language. He lived in Arizona, at the edge of the Sonoran Desert, and he loved the hot, dry days and the cold nights. The clean sky. The lack of plant life. The paucity of people. The birds that liked to hide away. It was a fact that he was not a birder. He was here to find the child. Even though it was his policy never to take custody cases, he had agreed because of the large sum offered, but now here he was in this dirty pueblo for the second time within a month, chasing after a child who might not exist. He had misstepped in coming here too early, just after the girl had kidnapped the child, and long before she would have made it home. But the couple had insisted, and so he'd arrived, and of course found nothing. The people of the village to whom he spoke were unhelpful. Everyone either shrugged or pretended not to understand. Even the few local police were unhelpful. The village, the climate, the police, the stray dogs—everything conspired against Derek Grima.

The following morning, early, a man, short and with a fey step and a lilting voice, appeared at his door and asked in fairly good English if he was Señor Grima.

He was. And who would this be?

My name is Santiago, the little man said. He bowed slightly. He might even have clicked his heels. Slightly comical.

Santiago said that if Señor Grima was looking for a child named Meja, then he, Santiago, was the one to help. For a certain amount, Santiago said, I can take you to her.

What amount? Grima asked.

Santiago gave a number and then ducked his head as if the asking price might be too exorbitant.

How do I know who you are? Grima asked.

I am Santiago. I can help you find the child.

Grima studied him. Now? he asked.

She has just arrived. With the girl named Íso. If we do not go today, you will miss her. Perhaps you would like to prepare, Santiago said. Shave, bathe, dress in your good clothes. When you are ready, I will take you to the child. You will check out, take your bags. Everything will happen quickly. Again, Santiago made a movement with his head, very appealing and convivial.

Grima stepped back into his room and did as Santiago had suggested. He shaved and showered, and then he dressed in black pants and slipped into his boots and lastly buttoned up his shirt. He took his passport and his wallet. His small valise. He had a phone, and the phone had a camera. He would take photos. He would hopefully retrieve the child. But of course everything was unknown here and unpredictable and shifty. The people were friendly but impervious. He might find himself on the verge of understanding, and then the clarity slipped away, like a fish that slips by in the shallows of a fast-flowing river. He missed the river near his home. He missed the certainty. He was tired.

They went to the pier by foot. As they walked, Santiago pointed out vistas, and he said in Spanish the names of the various sights as they passed. He said that he was a carpenter by trade. Business was slow. Therefore a livelihood must be made by other means. No? He said that most recently he had built windows for a customer but the customer had been unhappy and had refused to pay. But that was not the worst of it. The customer had spoken poorly of him, had spread stories of his incompetence. This we cannot do, take away a man's honour. He stopped speaking and took Grima's elbow and guided him down the hill towards the pier.

They boarded a boat that could easily have held thirty. But there were only three: Grima, Santiago, and the driver, a young man who appeared to know Santiago well. His name was Daniel. The crossing was rough. The wind was high, the water choppy. It was impossible to speak and so they sat, Santiago and Grima, in the middle of the boat, and Grima watched the landscape and the sky and he viewed the volcanoes in three directions, and though there were other boats on the lake, it seemed that they were all alone.

They landed on a solitary beach where an egret watched imperiously and then lifted into the wind and floated away.

What is this place? Grima asked. He saw no habitation and little indication that there was a nearby village.

Santiago pointed up the hill. A short walk, he said. It is better that we arrive unannounced.

Daniel had joined them. He held a machete with which he would clear a path. He led and Santiago took up the rear. Grima was not in the best of shape and soon he was panting and breathing heavily. They paused on a promontory and Santiago produced a sweating bottle of water and handed it to Grima. He took it and he drank copiously, aware of the heat, and his own thirst, and at the back of his brain, a slight ticking of alarm.

They walked on. The light above grew brighter. The sun bore down. Grima thought that he had chosen poorly. And then he thought that he must now trust. And then he panicked. And breathed. Don't be foolish, he thought. But of course he was foolish. And he had chosen poorly. He thought that he might die up here on this hill, with the indifferent volcanoes looking down on his body, and with the lake lying like a jewel below. And he thought that even if he could understand what was to come to pass, he was powerless to help himself. He was breathing heavily again, and he was very thirsty. When he asked for more water, Santiago smiled pitifully and said that he was sorry, but it was all gone. It is finished, he said.

THREE months after Señor Grima disappeared, the police arrived and at the behest of their superiors in the city they questioned the owner of the hotel, and they questioned Santiago, the owner of the carpintería, and they questioned Señora Perdido, the proprietress of a small tienda that carried expensive products desired by foreigners. Discovering nothing, they concluded that Señor Grima's existence, like every human being's, was ephemeral and elusive. In any case, they were not being paid anything extra for this inquiry, and so they returned to their work in the city.

At that time, Íso and Meja were staying with an aunt from her father's side who lived in a northern village, a three-hour bus ride from the lake. Once a week Señora Perdido closed her tienda and travelled north to see her daughter and her granddaughter. Meja was on the verge of walking now. She was fat and happy. Her legs were perhaps a little too chubby. She might be overeating. She always recognized her abuelita. Señora Perdido was sad when she had to say goodbye. But she was happy for Íso.

THE seasons passed. Íso moved home to live with her mother. During the week, she studied at the university in the city and her mother cared for Meja. On weekends she returned to the village and on Saturdays she sometimes walked up to her uncle's carpintería, where they visited while Meja played in the sawdust and collected blocks of ceiba. There were still times, when Íso sat in her mother's tienda on a Sunday and she heard the sound of an approaching motorcycle, that she turned her head as if foreseeing his arrival. It was a habit that she would never grow out of, though the leaping of her heart, and the curiosity and the fear, would ultimately disappear. Her memory was fierce. Her spirit fiercer.

And then, during one of the rainy seasons, with a suddenness that was unanticipated, the water of the lake began to rise. It rose ten feet within a month. The rains did not stop and the lake continued to rise. Those who had been imprudent and built their houses close to the shores witnessed the water lap at their doors, and then cover the windows, and eventually all that remained to be seen were the peaks of those houses. Certain villagers, one a Tz'utujil bonesetter in his late nineties, simply shrugged and said that it was the way of the lake. This happened every fifty years. The temperament of nature was both predictable and surprising.

The clinic at Ixchel was threatened. Albañiles were hired to build concrete walls that would hold back the water. Soon, the clinic and its surrounding gardens came to resemble a castle circled on three sides by a vast moat. The high walls hid the panorama of the lake and what remained was a view of the sky, and the volcano Tolimán, which on windy days was obscured by the crown of clouds swirling around its summit.

Fewer and fewer women arrived to take the waters. Eventually, the clinic was shut down. The abandoned buildings fell into disrepair. One afternoon, during a powerful wind, a retaining wall gave way and the water poured in. The paths and the gardens were the first to disappear, and then the clay baldosas along the interior walkway flooded, and then the pools were overwhelmed, and then the wide hall that led to the birthing rooms was covered. The jacaranda trees were the last to go, along with the paja roofs and peaks of the birthing chambers.

All has vanished. These days the site is rumoured to have an abundance of fish that grow to the size of a child's hand and swim in schools amongst the ruins. The waters are teeming. At night, the fishermen come and sit in their cayucos and cast their nets, their head lanterns lighting up the remains of Ixchel, which lie buried beneath the lake.

# ACKNOWLEDGEMENTS

THANK YOU TO MY EARLY READERS OF THIS NOVEL—TOM, Larry and Lyne, Ellen and Adrian, Roger and his father, Eddie (who at 103 is the oldest reader I have), and of course Mary, my first reader. I am grateful to Randi Lott, who worked as a nurse and midwife in Santiago de Atitlán, and who generously answered every one of my questions. Thanks to Nikaela, and to her son Gil, who was my most immediate entry into the world of an infant. To my agents, Ellen Levine and Alexa Stark, thank you. And finally, thank you to Iris Tupholme, my wonderful editor.

# About the Author

David Bergen is the award-winning author of eight previous novels and a collection of short stories. Among his acclaimed works are *The Time in Between*, which won the Scotiabank Giller Prize; *The Matter with Morris*, which was a finalist for the Giller Prize, the winner of the Carol Shields Winnipeg Book Award and the Margaret Laurence Award for Fiction, and a finalist for the International IMPAC Dublin Literary Award; *The Age of Hope*, which was a finalist for Canada Reads; and his much praised latest novel, *Leaving Tomorrow*. Bergen lives in Winnipeg.